for Peg,

With best
wishes

Katy Gallison

7/31/87

THE DEATH TAPE

Also by Kate Gallison

Unbalanced Accounts

THE DEATH TAPE

KATE GALLISON

LITTLE, BROWN AND COMPANY BOSTON TORONTO

FIRST EDITION

Library of Congress Cataloging-in-Publication Data

Gallison, Kate.
The death tape.

I. Title.
PS3557.A414D4   1987   813'.54   87-3855
ISBN 0-316-30299-6

RRD VA

Designed by Patricia Dunbar

Published simultaneously in Canada
by Little, Brown & Company (Canada) Limited

PRINTED IN THE UNITED STATES OF AMERICA

THE DEATH TAPE

ONE

OSWALD BADGER stood naked on the cold concrete floor of the men's comfort station of the Bosnian-American Social Club. Laughter and softball noises came faintly from the picnic ground. A pale, balding man with little breasts looked back at him from the mirror; he puffed his chest out, tightening the muscles of his belly. Almost fondly Badger gazed at the trousers and shirt in his hand, a very ordinary pair of khaki trousers, a completely inoffensive short-sleeved white shirt, and then stuffed the clothing into the trash container.

Then he put on a pair of red boxer bathing trunks, picked up his gym bag, and went out into the sunny afternoon.

Nick Magaracz stepped out of the stall.

The Bosnian-American Social Club is on a hill north of Trenton, New Jersey. It isn't fancy, but the grounds are very good for picnics, and the club rents them out for office parties. The Taxation picnic was there this year, Magaracz's first office picnic since Ethel quit working to have Amy. He himself was serving out his six-month trial period as Enforcement Investigation Trainee.

By virtue of being a veteran he had gone to the top

of the list when he passed the Civil Service test, and now Nick Magaracz was doing what he had sworn never to do, working full-time for the State. It wasn't so bad. Like Ethel said, it was a steady paycheck, and lots of days off. And anyway he wasn't going to do it forever. Industrial espionage was what he was going to get into next, just as soon as he finished being a state worker. He still had all the stuff from his old office (torn down last month by the city) — his oak desk, the stuffed bass, little Amy's clown painting, everything, all waiting in the attic for the day when he had his new act together.

But not yet.

The warm bosom of Mother Civil Service was not easy to leave. Self-employment had been great, his own boss, keeping his own hours, but until Amy's teeth were out of braces he needed the state dental insurance.

"Clothes in the trash basket," he said to himself, finding no room for his paper towel. He pulled them out. There were things in the pockets: keys, money, a gasoline credit card in the name of Oswald Badger, and a laminated permit for State Parking Area Six, the most convenient lot in Trenton after Area One, which was reserved for state legislators and big ma-hoffs.

He stared at the Area Six parking permit for a long time, wrestling with his better nature.

Outside on the picnic grounds, merriment held sway. The softball game was at the top of the seventh inning. The quoits competition was heating up, with sounds of cheers and clanging metal. Draft beer flowed like water, and water flowed as well, as young girls filled balloons at the faucet in the ladies' room and rushed out to cast them at the revelers. In the bushes a couple was necking. Ethel Magaracz felt like an outsider.

Ethel knew nobody there except for the two old Bosnian ladies who were cooking the food at the refreshment booth, friends of hers from Saint Joachim's Church. They grumbled about the state of the Bosnian Club while Ethel waited for the sausage to finish cooking.

"Those men should be doing this, not me," said Maria Hedervary. "At my age."

"Now, Maria," said her sister Ruza.

"What men?" said Ethel.

"The other club members," Ruza said. A crowd came up demanding corn, and inquiring after the state of the sausage.

"Not cooked yet," said Ruza, while a surly Maria doled out the steaming ears of corn.

"My dear," said Ruza Hedervary when the last of them had taken their food and gone away, "you've no idea how fine this club was once." Ethel grunted sympathetically, causing the old ladies to launch into a recitation of the complete history of the Bosnian-American Social Club, which had been established in 1908 as the Bosnian-American Social, Sick and Death Benefit Society by their father and a number of other movers and shakers of Trenton's Bosnian community. They recited this history in the intervals between dishing up hot dogs, ears of corn, and platefuls of Bosnian potato salad to the thronging picnickers, and wound up with a denunciation of the club's president.

As Ethel tried to follow their story, a paunchy little man in red undershorts brushed past, carrying a gym bag. Ethel started, then realized it was a bathing suit

5

he was wearing, not underwear. He seemed to be heading for the clubhouse, about fifty yards up the hill.

"Only half Bosnian on his mother's side," Maria was saying, with a gesture toward the clubhouse, a long, low clapboard building that had seen better days. "There he is now, may he roast." A man in a suit and tie was on the porch. For a moment he seemed to be watching them; then he turned and went inside. The one in the bathing suit had disappeared.

"Who?" Ethel said.

Maria sniffed. "Herman Eckes. The president. He's the one who made the club what it is today, the more shame to him."

"Why is he the president?" said Ethel. "Can't you get him out? How did he get into the club?"

"His mother belonged," said Ruza. "She was a Princip."

"A what?"

"A Princip. It was her maiden name. Gavrilo Princip was Herman Eckes's great-uncle."

"And who was Gavrilo Princip?" said Ethel.

"My dear," said Maria darkly, "he murdered Archduke Ferdinand in Sarajevo. It was the start of the Great War."

"So after his mother passed away," Ruza continued, "Herman packed the club with all those other people, and before we knew it we were outvoted. Now they want to raise the dues again."

"But none of them will help you with the cooking," said Ethel.

"No, they're keeping out of sight," Maria said. "They do that when there's work to be done. But you can bet they're around someplace. I think I will quit, just

6

for the satisfaction of watching those louts try to cook a sausage. Would you like one, by the way, Ethel dear? They're done now." They smelled delicious.

"Yes, please, Maria. And a couple for Nick. Ah. Here he comes." Her husband was approaching from the men's room, walking fast, looking all around at the crowd. "Here I am, Nick," she called to him. "Come get your sausage, it's ready."

"Hi," he said. "Did you see a fellow without any pants come by here a minute ago?"

"If you mean the little man in the red bathing suit," Ethel said, "I saw him going over toward the clubhouse."

"Bathing suit. Of course," he said. "He's headed for the dunk tank, I bet. Must be drunk. That would explain it. Do you have any horseradish?"

"We certainly do," said Ruza.

"Okay, put some horseradish on my sausage, please, Ethel, and meet me over by the tank. I'm going to look around some more for that guy."

"What's going on?" Ethel said.

"I'm not sure," he said, leaving.

"Your husband is always so mysterious," Ruza sighed. "How interesting it must be to be married to a detective."

"Yes," said Ethel. "So, tell me, what would you do with yourselves if you left the Bosnian Club?" She started gathering up her food.

"Plenty," Maria said, fixing Ethel with a haughty stare. "Plenty. I might even take up shooting again. I was quite good, you know. There's a glass case in the clubhouse full of my cups."

Ruza shuddered. "Oh, those awful guns of hers."

"I could put a hole in the eye of a fly at thirty paces,"

Maria boasted. "That was something men respected."

"I bet they did," said Ethel. More people came to get their lunch. Ethel picked up her plates of sausage, corn, and potato salad, balanced them carefully in her arms, and carried them away. Nick was not by the dunk tank.

These sausages will be too cold even for Nick, thought Ethel, and she stood on tiptoe to look around for him. He was nowhere to be seen. As usual.

A wet young woman in a T-shirt and shorts was climbing back up to the dunk-tank seat.

"Three for a dollar," called the young fellow selling dunk-tank tickets. "Only one dollar for three shots at dunking the lovely lady in the tank."

The lovely lady sat on a perch behind a net to keep from getting hit by stray baseballs. Below her waited a tank of muddy, leafy water, four feet deep. Firemen had pumped it out of the creek.

One of the men stepped up, paid his dollar, and fired three baseballs in rapid succession at the trigger, a metal disk about ten inches in diameter on the end of a lever. The first two balls went into the net, but the third connected. *Thwop! Thwop! Thwang!* Down went the lovely lady, her good-sport smile frozen to her face. Water splashed over the sides of the tank.

The water-balloon girls came charging through the crowd and plastered the ball-thrower a good one. Everybody was wet. Ethel stepped back to save herself a drenching.

The barker was handed a note. "I have been asked to announce that the sack race begins in five minutes," he said. "Everyone entered in the sack race please report to the sack-race location." Some of the people began to move toward the field with the sacks.

8

A little breeze was starting up. The barker called out again, "Three shots for a dollar. Three chances to drop the gentleman into the tank of water."

The man in the red trunks climbed out on the perch. Ethel noticed that he had remarkably tiny feet. Breezes ruffled the strips of hair he had combed across his bald spot. He smiled a strange self-contained little smile, as though the fact that he was about to be dunked in a tub of cold muddy water was very far from his thoughts.

Nick popped up at Ethel's elbow. " 'Zat my sausage?" he asked her.

"It's cold," she said. He grabbed it and bit into it.

"Just right," he said with his mouth full. "Yum."

She said, "How you can eat cold sausage — !"

People were buying balls to throw at the dunk tank. "Going to try your luck, Nick?" she said.

"Naw. I'm saving my dollars for the girls. When they fall in they get their T-shirts wet, right?"

"Oh, Nick, you're terrible." *Thwop! Thwop!* went the baseballs, and still the little man kept his seat.

"Excuse me," Nick called up to the man. "Would your name be Oswald Badger?"

The man looked down at him. "Why, yes," he replied.

Then, *thwang!* somebody had hit the dunk-tank trigger.

It was almost like a slow-motion movie, the little perch tilting and letting him slip off, the smile fading to a look of dismay as he dropped into the brown leafy water.

Splash! and a wave came sloshing over the side of the tank. Mr. Badger's head sank beneath the surface.

Clapping and tittering from the crowd.

But when his face reappeared above the water it was contorted with pain and fear. Mr. Badger was gasping and thrashing. Two men helped him out of the tank. "Heart attack," he said, and fell on his face in the grass.

Ethel stood aghast as others pushed forward to see or help out. Some offered to give poor Mr. Badger CPR, having taken courses in it from Civil Service. Then the man who had been on the clubhouse porch came out of the crowd.

"I'm a doctor," he said. "Step back, please, and give him air."

Mr. Badger was twitching, unconscious, and blue; he was obviously in terrible trouble. The doctor leaned over and loosened his tongue, to be sure he wasn't choking, mopped his brow, and covered him with a dry beach towel. A couple of the men went running toward the clubhouse to call the Lifemobile, but Badger breathed his last, a horrible rattle, before they reached the clubhouse steps.

"I'm sorry," said the doctor, standing up and wiping his hands. "He's gone. There's nothing I can do for him. It must have been the shock of the water."

TWO

OSWALD BADGER left a lot of work behind, as any good bureaucrat would. His second in command, Roger Diefnagel, set to work Monday morning to clean out Badger's desk and take care of his most urgent tasks.

It was depressing. Certain things could be consigned to a cardboard box without thinking about them — half-empty packs of breath mints, the catalogue from Abe's War Surplus — but what to do with such things as the World's Greatest Boss coffee mug, or the pen and pencil set with the engraved stand, presented by an admiring staff when Badger was promoted? Badger had no family that anyone knew of. Diefnagel stuck them in a plastic bag and turned his attention to the things that weren't personal.

Like this computer printout. But what the hell was it? A job name, a date, and a list of names, addresses, large amounts of money, and mysterious codes of some sort. Most of the names were crossed out in black marker.

Badger's secretary, Lora Watson, wasn't in, so he couldn't ask her about it. He would ask the data processing input/output clerk.

"Oh, yeah," said Rory the clerk, when he got him

on the phone. "The death tape job. That's a report."

"What does it report?" said Diefnagel.

"I dunno. You'll have to ask the analyst."

The analyst was Marcia Hoover. She came to his office, breathless as usual, with a brown cardboard envelope under her arm bearing the job ID number, and tried to explain it to him.

The death tape job, as everyone seemed to call it, was a matching of two sets of data. One, the death tape, held the names of everyone who had died in the State of New Jersey in a given year, together with their Social Security numbers and assorted other items of information. The other, the bank tape, was a record of accounts kept in banks in the state in that same year, the amount of money in each account, and the name and Social Security number of each depositor. The death tape job took these two files of data and made a report.

"A report," he said. "Right." He spread it out before her. "What are these names and figures?"

"Well," she said, "since you first asked me about it over the phone, I went through the program to see what it actually *does*. It's not very well documented; it was what they call quick and dirty. And then, it's unstructured, and it's hard for me to read unstructured COBOL, I was trained on structured, so it was kind of —"

"Can you give me any idea what this report is about?" said Diefnagel.

"Basically, it's a list of dead people who had over twenty-five thousand dollars in the bank."

"These are their names, addresses, and Social Security numbers, then," said Diefnagel.

"Right," said Marcia. "And this is the bank code, and how much money was in each account."

"What is this date?"

"That comes from the death tape. It's the date of death."

"Thanks," said Diefnagel. "This should prove very helpful."

As for the crossed-out names, Diefnagel supposed that Oswald Badger had asked Lora to look them up to see whether their inheritance taxes were paid. Diefnagel looked up two himself that he was able to read through the marker ink and yes, the heirs had paid. And as for the others . . .

As for the others, there existed here a clear possibility of delinquency. As there were thirty-two of them, all with sums in the bank in excess of twenty-five thousand, it seemed to Diefnagel like a good thing to pursue. With discretion, of course; the Attorney General had ruled more than once that any use of Social Security numbers for other than statistical purposes was illegal.

Perhaps Badger had moved on it already. Taking the report in hand, Diefnagel called Arthur Pacewick, chief of Tax Enforcement Investigation, on the eighth floor. Was his group doing anything along the lines of an inheritance tax investigation?

"No," said Pacewick. "Are we supposed to be?"

"I wasn't sure," said Diefnagel. "That is, I wasn't sure whether Oswald had got you started on it yet. If I give you a list of names this afternoon, can you put somebody on it?"

"Sure," said Pacewick. "Matter of fact, Magaracz is free this week."

                    *   *   *

Arthur Pacewick didn't like Nick Magaracz.

He didn't know why, really. The two had a lot in
common. They were both family men, and Korean
veterans; they both had been private investigators,
although Pacewick had worked for a huge multina-
tional agency when Magaracz was reporting to no one
but himself.

But there the resemblance ended.

Nick Magaracz was of Trenton, and Pacewick feared
and hated the town, though he believed it was the last
place left where he could get a job. Nick seemed to
swim through Trenton like a rat through its native
sewer. He knew everybody in town. Nor did he fear,
as Pacewick did, to get fired; he looked forward to it,
as he often told anyone who would listen, for an excuse
to resume his madcap existence as a P.I. It made Pacewick uneasy to have such a free spirit under his command.

Once Pacewick took his fractious subordinate to
lunch in an attempt to improve their working relationship. Nick recommended the Neon Bar, a four-
block walk through the middle of town. In those four
sunny blocks Nick greeted and was greeted by three
quarters of the people they met, people of all ages,
races, and economic conditions. Some were derelicts,
drunk on the curbstone; another was Mayor Arthur
Holland himself; yet another was Hester Porcineau,
octogenarian heiress to the Porcineau meat-packing
fortune, chairman of the board of Porcineau Indus-
tries, the richest woman in Mercer County.

The old lady was standing beside her black Lincoln
town car shaking a parking meter and cursing. When
she saw them coming, she said, "Nick Magaracz! For

                        14

God's sake give me a dime!" He did. She put it in the meter, and turned the crank, whereupon the needle ticked over and registered half an hour. "Half these meters are defective," she remarked. "It's enough to make your piles come down."

"And bleed," Nick agreed amiably, and moved on, without introducing Arthur Pacewick. He was dying to ask how Magaracz knew her, but to do so would be to lose face.

When they got to the Neon it proved to be exactly the kind of place where Pacewick would expect to find a guy like Nick Magaracz. Pacewick hated it. The bartender greeted Magaracz as an old friend and gave them the table by the window.

Their working relationship was not improved. Magaracz continued to be a discomfort, like an unsatisfactory pair of shoes. Pacewick felt that unspoken wisecracks were hovering all the time on Magaracz's lips. He could see one now, as Magaracz looked up at him from the work spread out on his desk.

"Here," Pacewick said, and gave him the green-striped computer printout that Roger Diefnagel had sent up. "I want you to track down as many of these people as you can. They're all dead. Start with the ones with the most money. Find out how many of their heirs have cheated on their inheritance tax."

THREE

THE HOUSE WHERE Gilmore Nash's widow lived was not very tidy and not very big. There were holes in the lawn, some with stainless steel spoons sticking out of them. A fifty-seven Studebaker with a big dent in the right rear fender was parked in the dirt driveway, light gray, wearing a failed inspection sticker. Nice car, if you like old cars, but rusty and needing a lot of work. The front windows of the house showed the wrong side of those Hindu bedspreads that the hippies used to like. Magaracz wondered what kind of person would answer the door.

He could have telephoned, but he wanted to catch her by surprise, check out the house, see if she seemed to be spending a lot of money, and like that.

The door opened. The woman who stood blinking at him was maybe thirty-five, pale, thin in jeans and a loose, full-sleeved shirt. Her red hair was pulled back tight from her face. Little curly bits of it got loose here and there and blew around.

"Yes?" she said.

"Mrs. Nash?" said Magaracz. The woman nodded. "My name is Nick Magaracz." He showed his badge. "I'm with the Bureau of Tax Enforcement. I'd like to talk to you for a minute, if it's okay."

"Please come in."

The parlor, like the front yard, had a look of young boys living in it, socks, little plastic men with ugly faces, fancy setups of tracks and cars. It smelled of cigarette butts.

"I hope you'll excuse the way the house looks," she said. "I've been at school since early this morning and I haven't had time to straighten up. Please sit down." She moved a little pair of sneakers and a half-eaten jelly sandwich to make room for him on the sofa. He sat. She perched on a chair.

She said, "How can I help you?" Her manner was very grave. Her eyes were round and blue. She didn't look like an expensive woman.

"You say you were at school," he said. "Are you a teacher?"

"Oh, no. A part-time student. And a part-time legal secretary. I work for Lockman, Lockman and Gould."

"I know of them," Magaracz said. He had done some divorce work for old Lockman in the days when you could make a buck that way.

There was a silence. She looked at him, as if to say, "It's your turn to talk." He waited for a minute to see if she would show any signs of guilt. She didn't.

"I won't beat around the bush, Mrs. Nash," he said. "Our records show that no tax has been paid on your husband's estate."

This seemed to take her completely by surprise. "On his . . . his what?"

"We have reason to believe that your husband, Gilmore Nash, left an estate worth many thousands of dollars. No tax has been paid on it."

She stared at him for a long time. "Mr. Magaracz," she said at last, "I wonder if you have a cigarette.

17

I was going to quit, but now I think I'd like one."

"Sure. Here," he said, producing a crumpled pack of stale filter cigarettes that he carried around with him. They were strong and smelly, not a nice cigarette for ladies, or men either for that matter, but he kept them for old times' sake and smoked one no oftener than once a month. That was one of the reasons he still had his health.

He lit one for her. She inhaled, without even coughing, and blew the smoke out through her nose.

Then she stood up, and before he could figure out what she was doing, unbuttoned her cuff, raised her arm, and let the sleeve fall to her shoulder.

"You see this?" she said. "That's as far as I'll ever be able to bend it. See the scar?" It was like an old war wound. "That's my legacy from Gilmore. The whole thing. How much of that would the State of New Jersey like to have?"

"What did he do?"

"I don't remember," she said. "I have gaps."

"Gee, I'd remember something like that," Magaracz said. "Maybe you ought to see somebody about it."

"Oh, right," she said. "Pay some shrink a hundred dollars an hour to help me remember Gilmore." She sat down, and sighed, and smoked some more. There wasn't any ashtray. She dropped the ashes in the back of a little dump truck. "I'm sorry," she said. "But I can't imagine where you got the idea that Gilmore had money."

Magaracz said, "The State computer. There was supposed to be a hundred and thirty thousand dollars in the bank."

"What an extraordinary thing."

"The tax on that, Mrs. Nash, comes to five thousand

18

two hundred dollars, if it went to you and your children. You can see why the State is interested."

She put the cigarette out on the cab of the truck and began to chew her thumb. "I'm interested myself," she said. "A hundred and thirty thousand dollars."

"Maybe you want to talk it over with your lawyer."

"No," she said, "I know about inheritance tax, Mr. Magaracz, and I'd pay it in an instant if I only had that money. But, you see, I don't. What bank did your computer say it was in? Maybe it's still there."

He named a large bank in downtown Trenton. "I'll stop off there on my way back to the office," he said, "and if they still have the money I'll give you a call."

"Thank you," she said. "But it has to be a mistake. I can't think where Gilmore would have . . . unless it belonged to one of his clubs. He belonged to a whole lot of clubs, everywhere we went. I still have his uniform from the Posse Comitatus. He was even an officer in the Bosnian Club, a vice-president, I think."

"The Bosnian-American Social Club?"

"Yes. It's down the road a couple of miles. You must have read about it in the paper last week, that poor man who had the heart attack in the tank."

"I was there at the picnic," Magaracz said.

"It must have been awful." She shuddered.

"Tragic," he agreed. "What would the Bosnians be doing with a hundred and thirty thousand dollars?"

She shrugged. "They were planning some improvements to the place. And then, there were things that they stockpiled."

"Frozen sausage? Or what?"

"I don't really know. There were conversations on the phone; I didn't hear very much. Listen, why don't

19

you ask the bank if they still have the money? I'll try to think of reasons why he might have been keeping it for someone else."

"Okay," he said.

She said, "I hope they have it. I hope it's mine, and I get to keep it. Scott and Henry could really use some new shoes."

"I hope so, too," said Magaracz. "You know, Nash is a funny name for a Bosnian. What did it used to be?"

"Always Nash," she said. "Hardly any of them are Bosnians anymore. There's only the two old sisters. If they're still alive. I haven't been to the club since Gilmore's death."

"Why not? With the children, and all. It's right down the road."

"The dues are very high. And I don't really like those people. They were Gilmore's friends."

"I'll call you as soon as I find out anything about the money," said Magaracz, leaving. In the car he suddenly thought: *What is the Posse Comitatus?*

In downtown Trenton there is a bar and restaurant where young men who are interested in each other like to meet. Woman state workers have lunch there too, sometimes, in crowds of five and six, giggling surreptitiously at the mannerisms of the waiters. The hamburgers are excellent, and not overpriced, and it is an okay place to eat lunch, although there are some strange rumors about what goes on in there after dark. The decor is astonishing, something between the main salon of the *Queen Mary* and the set of a Fred Astaire and Ginger Rogers movie.

It was there that Rory Valentine, now a habitué,

waited to meet his friend and sometime lover, Ace Jeder.

He nursed his third beer and watched the door. People coming in for lunch were silhouetted against the noon brightness, but nobody with the particular way of holding his body that Ace had, a strange mixture of grace and awkwardness. To watch him still made the hair stand up on Rory's arms. There he was now.

But not alone. There was another man with him. Ace was dressed in his customary outfit, camouflage pants and a black T-shirt, and over that the hooded orange sweatshirt that said "Bergenfield High" on the back, the one that gave him such a curious birdlike appearance when the hood was pulled up. It was his nose, Rory reflected, or maybe his thin shoulders. Whatever. He took another belt of beer and wondered again who this guy with him was.

"Rory!" said the Ace, with a toothy smile, as he pulled up another chair to the table. "This is Dr. Herman Eckes. Dr. Eckes, Rory Valentine. I wanted the two of you to meet."

"Why?" said Rory, eyeballing the other man, gray-haired and grim-jawed in a threadbare Brooks Brothers suit. What was he doing with this person? He was strange-looking. In fact the pair of them might have been crazies out on a day pass from Trenton Psychiatric.

But the Ace refused to acknowledge his rudeness, and breezily ordered another round. "Dr. Eckes changed my life," he said to Rory. "We think he's a very great man. I wanted you to know him."

The great man grunted, and downed half his beer at a swallow. "I'm very pleased to meet you, Rory," he said. "Ace, here, has told me a great deal about you. Tell me, do you know where the men's room is in this place?" He gazed around the room with faint distaste, almost as if he'd never been in a gay bar before.

Rory pointed the way, and the older man went off to the men's room. *Who is that guy?* Rory wanted to ask, but what he said was "When can I see you?"

"I'll give you a call," said the Ace. "I have to work on something tonight."

"I'll bet you do."

"It's not what you think," said the Ace. "There's nothing between us. He's my political mentor."

"Whatever the fuck that is." Rory drank up the beer, his fourth, and began to feel it.

In his soft voice the Ace made a little speech about freedom, and fitness for leadership, and how the government was usurping powers. He made beautiful gestures; his hands and forearms were elegant. "It's a matter of correcting injustice, Rory, of putting things right. I have to help."

"Yeah, right."

Dr. Eckes rejoined them, casting apprehensive glances over his shoulder. "That waiter just said the strangest thing to me," he complained.

"You can help us, Rory," the Ace was saying. "You can tell us the password that goes with the log-on code you told me about last week."

"Do what?" said Rory.

"Then I can call up and borrow the State's mainframe to do some stuff I have to get done, and I'll have tomorrow evening free. We can be together."

"This is for the course you're taking, right?" said Rory. "This is for school."

"Right. I need a COBOL compiler."

"N-four-P-eight," he replied, and the doctor wrote it down.

"And there's something I need to know, too," the doctor said. "I was hoping you could tell me what the State had in the way of security software." He smiled at Rory expectantly.

"I couldn't say," said Rory.

"Who could?" Dr. Eckes pressed.

"Consultants," he said. The beer was getting to him; soon he would have to get back to work. "It was all set up by consultants."

"What consultants?" said the Ace.

"Hm?"

"You mentioned consultants," the doctor said.

"Who does their consulting?" said the Ace.

"Werfels and DiTresso," he answered at last.

"Oh," they said.

"What did you want to know for?"

Speaking both at once, the men answered. Dr. Eckes said, "No reason," and the Ace said, "My father needs some computer consultants for his company."

Magaracz went to the bank. The money was long gone. The manager, intimidated by Magaracz's T-man credentials, volunteered that it had been drawn out, all at once, on a certain date, by the account holder himself.

Magaracz drew a folded page of green-striped paper from his wallet and looked at it. "The date that Mr. Nash died," he said, "was the day before that."

"Couldn't be," said the manager. "It's right here in the records. Date stamps don't lie, Mr. McRats."

Magaracz gazed out through the manager's glass

23

partition into the lobby. Lunchtime on the first of the month, and all the pensioners and welfare mothers were thronging to the counters, crowding among the state workers, who had also just been paid. How could the tellers know one face, among all those faces?

"Could somebody have impersonated Nash?" Magaracz asked the manager. "Forged his name?"

The manager sighed. "It happens from time to time," he said. "I won't pretend it doesn't. But if that were the case, why didn't anyone come forward to complain?"

"Who?" said Magaracz. "Nash himself was dead. Maybe you have a videotape of the person who cashed this, and we can see who it was."

"We only keep them for a year," the manager said. "But with all due respect, I really do think you should check the date of death again. It has to be a mistake. You see, here is the signature. It's no different from the others."

Sure enough, the signature appearing on the microfilm copy of Nash's withdrawal slip was just like all the rest, allowing for the small differences that naturally occur between two specimens of the same person's writing.

Magaracz had a cheese dog at the Dixie Lunch and went over to Human Services. There a number of bureaucrats and clerks gave him a hard time. In the end they reluctantly plumbed the depths of their filing system and produced a true copy of Gilmore Nash's death certificate. From this document the original data had been keyed in to make up the death tape.

Cause of death, congestive heart failure; attending

physician, Herman Eckes, D.O.; date of death, same as the report said. No mistake on the date.

Unless the doctor had made a mistake.

He called Monica Nash and filled her in. She was disappointed about the money.

Yes, very disappointed about the money, but of course she really hadn't expected any. Gilmore would hardly have left his own money where his archenemy, the government, could find it out, still less where Monica might get it if he died. Gilmore knew all about banks and the records they kept. But then, with Gilmore, there was no telling why he did anything.

The weirdness of Gilmore. There was no end to it even in death.

As long as he was alive, Monica never fully realized how much she hated Gilmore. They say you don't appreciate people until they're gone. With Gilmore it was quite the reverse. When he died it was like novocaine wearing off after some dreadful procedure. She fully felt the pain of his horribleness. For months she kept thinking, *Oh, my God, was he really like that? Did he really do those things?* Then she finally realized.

He was truly gone. He wasn't ever coming back.

She went to the hairdresser and got a perm. They put a rinse on the gray streak. She went back to school part-time. She met Kevin Mandelbaum.

Kevin was wonderful. He was supportive, and respectful, and gentle. He knew how to cook, and how to juggle five oranges, or three eggs. He could talk baseball knowledgeably with the children. He taught Henry to pitch. He never hit her. He was heaven in bed. It was eerie.

She couldn't believe her luck.

Especially after Gilmore. What horror. From time to time it seemed to Monica even now that she smelled him in the house.

The first night she spent with Kevin in her own bed, he curled up after they made love and slept all night as sound as a rock. Monica slept badly. She had a vivid nightmare of Gilmore, walking slowly up the stairs, clump, clump.

Bright yellow light shone under the door, showing his feet returned from the dead in thick brown shoes, waiting. Kevin was fast asleep. She held her breath for a long time.

In the morning nothing was out there, no footprints in graveyard mud, or ashes (Gilmore had been cremated), nor even in brimstone. No cloven hoofprints were burned into the hall runner. And yet . . .

There were nights when she went to bed all alone and seemed to smell Gilmore in the bedclothes, even though she washed them over and over and hung them out in the sun. She would lie all night with her eyes open. There were days when she brought in the mail and the envelopes looked funny.

"Boys, have you been opening my mail?"

"No, Mom."

"No, Mom."

Sometimes she would go down in the basement and the washer-dryer would be radiating a spectral warmth. Or she would come home from work, open the door, and think she smelled cigars.

"Maybe I'm going crazy," she said to herself. Or maybe Gilmore's presence was here, in this house.

FOUR

MAGARACZ HAD NO luck finding a Dr. Herman Eckes in the Physicians and Surgeons section of the Greater Trenton *Yellow Pages*. He was more successful with the Posse Comitatus. The reference librarian at the New Jersey State Library turned up an article from the *New York Times* describing them as a radical right-wing organization that had been causing trouble in the West.

Uniforms? They dressed like sheriffs. They crashed meetings of local governing bodies and made mock citizens' arrests. A number of them were in prison for kidnapping or tax evasion.

They hated to be taxed.

Since it was a nice afternoon for a ride, Magaracz decided to take a run out to the Bosnian Club to find out what they knew about Nash's hundred and thirty thou.

Tax revolt. Death and taxes.

Halfway there he thought, *I should have asked about Eckes at the library. Maybe he's been in the papers, too.*

The guard at the front gate was the same bony little fellow who had collected their tickets at the picnic, though Magaracz didn't remember him wearing a brown shirt. What did the Bosnians do for fun, Magaracz wondered, when they weren't catering picnics?

"I'm here to talk to somebody about some money," Magaracz said. "I'm from the State Department of Taxation." He flashed his badge. The man gaped at him.

"Is there somebody I could talk to?" Magaracz said, still being friendly. "About the club's finances and stuff."

The guard grunted. There was a phone in the little booth. He picked it up and said a few words into it. Sticking his head out of the booth, he said to Magaracz, "Whaddeya want, specifically? The doc says to ask you."

"It's about Gilmore Nash, specifically," said Magaracz. The guy's reaction was gratifying; he took a coughing fit, and almost dropped the phone.

Magaracz thought, *I must be onto something.*

The guard drew his head back into the booth, like a scrawny little turtle, and mumbled into the phone some more. "Go on in," he said finally. "Dr. Eckes will talk to you."

"Thanks." Magaracz set off up the path to the clubhouse, whistling tunelessly. Dr. Eckes. Nice. Two birds with one stone. Maybe he could wrap up the case right here, and go home early to Ethel.

The club was deserted except for the gatekeeper and a big-nosed kid with hair in his eyes trimming the grass around the driveway. Where were all the Bosnians? Long gone, Magaracz would have said, if not for those two friends of Ethel's, the Hedervary sisters. But they didn't seem to be here either.

The man in the gray suit standing on the clubhouse porch was none other than the one who had attended Oswald Badger's untimely departure. Fifty-five or sixty, slim, good-looking in a Nordic sort of way, with an iron-gray crew cut, he held his hands clasped behind his back and rocked backward and forward on his toes, waiting for Magaracz to climb the creaky steps.

Magaracz hated him on sight. Something about the doctor's appearance was deeply offensive to him. Was it his smile, a bleak baring of even white teeth like tombstones? Or was it the way he rocked? He had an air of having just changed out of an SS uniform.

"Dr. Herman Eckes?" said Magaracz.

Dr. Eckes put his right hand out, still with the smile. "Yes, I'm Dr. Eckes," he said, grasping Magaracz by the paw. "And you are — ?"

"Magaracz. Special agent. My card." The State of New Jersey had made up cards for him when he went to work as a T-man. They were classy, with the State Seal in one corner, blue and gold. When he was a private detective Magaracz had always meant to get cards, but never did. Anyway the clientele he used to deal with didn't expect them. He wondered what this doctor's racket was.

The doctor read his card, pocketed it, and grinned all the harder. "We'll be more comfortable in my office, Mr. Mog . . ."

"Magaracz. It rhymes with 'pots.' "

"My office is through here to the right." He ushered Magaracz through the wooden screen door. It was held with a spring and when he let it go it went *spang!* and all the hardware rattled. The clubhouse's main room seemed like a mountain lodge, full of graying wicker furniture, tables with old *National Geographic* magazines piled on them, and tattered pillows embroidered by Bosnian ladies a long time ago.

Dr. Eckes opened the door to his office, a room not

29

much bigger than a closet that held three tall filing cabinets, two chairs, and a modest desk. The picture that hung across from the desk was a late Victorian etching of a wild mountain landscape. Probably the mountains of Bosnia. Magaracz imagined reaching up and turning it over to reveal on the back a portrait of Adolf Hitler.

"If you'll sit down," said the doctor, settling himself behind the desk, "I'll try to answer any questions you might have." He leaned back and steepled his fingers. Magaracz noticed with revulsion that he polished his nails.

"Okay," said the detective. "How come a doctor has an office in a social club?" It wasn't what he had come to find out, but it was the question on his mind.

"Oh, ha, ha," said the doctor. "This isn't my professional office. That's in Conshohocken, Pennsylvania. This is the office of the president of the Bosnian-American Social Club, in which capacity I am presently serving."

"You don't practice medicine in New Jersey?"

The doctor looked pained. "Not anymore."

"Lost your license," Magaracz guessed.

"The State of New Jersey is way out of touch with modern medical practice," the doctor said. Magaracz took out his notebook and made a little note to go look up what wonderful modern practice it was that had cost Dr. Eckes his license.

"But you were practicing medicine in New Jersey when you signed a death certificate for Gilmore Nash," Magaracz said, "about a year and a half ago."

"Yes," said the doctor. "Poor Gilmore." He looked even more pained, and massaged his eyebrows.

30

"I take it that Mr. Nash was a personal friend."

"Yes, he was, Mr. Magaracz, which made it all the sadder. He collapsed and died right here in the club, after a number of strenuous laps around the field. None of us were aware of his heart condition."

Magaracz thought, *For a social club, this place is pretty unhealthy.* Maybe it was the sausage. All that cholesterol. "And you were here on the scene," said Magaracz. *Like you were with Badger.* How was he able to treat Oswald Badger, with no license? If he treated him. Something very fishy was going on here.

"There was nothing I could do. He was gone in a matter of minutes."

"Except to sign the death certificate."

"Except, as you say, to sign the death certificate. Poor Gilmore."

"There couldn't have been any mistake."

The doctor stared at him. "Mistake? What do you mean?"

"I mean, like, you're sure he was really dead, and he really died when you said he did on the death certificate, and all that."

The doctor said coldly, "Mr. Magaracz, I'm a professional man."

"Yeah," said Magaracz. "I was a professional man myself, Dr. Eckes, before I got to be a state worker. I know how it is. But there wasn't any doubt in your mind about Nash."

"I would never have signed a death certificate if there had been any doubt."

"Couldn't have been a case of catalepsy, I guess they call it, or one of those things people get where they seem to be dead but aren't."

"Gilmore Nash was dead, Mr. Magaracz. There was no heartbeat, no breathing, and in fact rigor mortis had begun to set in before I left him."

"Where did you leave him?"

"At Batt's Funeral Home."

Batt's, Magaracz wrote. Maybe there was something fishy there. "Then what?"

"Then he was cremated."

"Cremated. Right."

"It was his wish," said the doctor.

"Right."

"His ashes were scattered to the four winds. He loved the out-of-doors."

"I see," said Magaracz. "Then one of the four winds must have blown him to the bank, because he came in the next day and drew out a hundred and thirty thousand dollars."

"What!"

"That's really why I came here," Magaracz said. "I mean, I was glad to see you, I was looking for you anyhow. But what I came here about was to ask somebody about the money. Nash's widow suggested it might belong to the Bosnian Club. Him being an officer and all."

"There must be some mistake," the doctor said.

"Right," said Magaracz. "That's what I figured. And that's what I told the bank. But they said date stamps don't lie, and they showed me this stuff with his signature. So I came to you."

"Ah." The doctor gnawed the knuckle of his thumb and gazed at the mountains of Bosnia, seeking perhaps for a message from the image of Hitler where his face (Magaracz was almost sure of it now) was turned to the wall. "Yes, I see your difficulty."

32

"The reason I'm checking on it is, we figure that somebody owes inheritance tax on that money."

"Of course," said the doctor. He stood up. "Mr. Magaracz, I wonder if you would mind giving me some time to examine my records. It may be that after all I did make a mistake on the date."

"How about the money?" said Magaracz. "Can you find out whether it had anything to do with the club?"

"I will examine the treasurer's records as well. You should be hearing from me within the week." A flicker of secret amusement crossed the doctor's face with this, but it was gone so fast that Magaracz almost thought he imagined it.

"I'd appreciate anything you could find out," the detective said. "Thanks for your time, Dr. Eckes." He put the notebook back in his pocket and left the club.

The tall guy with the nose was nowhere in sight when Magaracz got outside. He gave the gatekeeper a nod, started his car, and went down the long gravel driveway to Route 29.

There would just be time before five o'clock to check out Dr. Eckes with the reference librarians at the State Library, a short walk from Parking Area Six. It was good to drive to Trenton knowing that he could park his car when he got there. Magaracz hummed a little tune. He had to slow down and be careful not to stop too short at the traffic lights, since there was a guy on a motorcycle trying to drive up his tailpipe.

The reference librarians were genial and helpful as always. They found many stories about the doctor in the New Jersey clippings file. Seeing how many times his name had appeared in the paper, Magaracz was surprised that he didn't remember ever reading or hearing about him. There were snippets about Herman Eckes, the Libertarian Party candidate for the State Assembly. Since he never ran in Magaracz's district, the detective was not surprised to have overlooked the doctor's political career, which was some years in the past and very short in any case.

And, yes, here was the expected account of how he was debarred from medical practice. A huge story, it must have broken sometime when Magaracz was out of town. Both local papers covered it.

The reporters were not in agreement about the doctor's character. One said Eckes was a humanitarian whose innovative treatments allowed his arthritic patients to lead almost normal lives. The other as much as called him a charlatan, a shameless quack who preyed on the sick. As for the details of his career, it seemed that shortly after World War II, which he spent in medical school, Dr. Eckes had returned to his home town of Trenton and set up practice, treating state workers with indifferent success at three dollars a visit. They all called him Three-Dollar Eckes.

As the years went by, Dr. Eckes began experimenting with certain combinations of drugs — on his patients, not on himself (*not a fool, anyway*, thought Magaracz) — and at last he developed a mixture that seemed to have a marked effect on certain kinds of ills, notably arthritis and a number of other similarly painful ailments. He built up a large practice. The drugs were administered by injection. Then came the hepatitis deaths, and the suspension of his license to practice medicine in the state.

Some time before that the doctor must have broken with the Libertarians; here in the file was a letter to the editor denouncing them as traitors to the right-wing cause, proto-socialists, and closet leftist sympathizers, signed Dr. Herman Eckes.

Another more surprising story told of how Dr. Herman Eckes was the sole survivor of a bear-hunting accident in Maine. Four men were drowned canoeing on the Allagash, and the fifth, the good doctor, was spared. *Bear hunting in a canoe?* thought Magaracz. He always heard the way you hunted bears was to sit over a pile of garbage, preferably the town dump of some northern backwater, and wait for the bears to come out at sundown. Nobody drowned on a bear hunt.

Anything on Gilmore Nash? The librarians had no file on such a person, either in the Jersey Reference section or on their on-line data base search systems. Obituaries were not routinely kept.

He started home, trying to figure the setup. Here was Eckes, a debarred doctor, an ex-pol of the right-wing stripe, apparently a survivor of the sort of stupid accident they like to write up as a heroic tale in *Yankee* magazine. Banished to Conshohocken. Yet at the Bosnian-American Social Club he carried on like he was the boss of something.

What the hell was this Eckes up to?

And who was that guy following Nick on a motor-cycle? Wasn't he the same one who had been behind him ever since he left the Bosnian Club?

Maybe Magaracz would look into it Monday. State workers always take the weekend off.

FIVE

 THREE TIMES THE bearded man pounded with the flat of his hand on the side of the Mill Hill semidetached town house.

It was broad daylight on the afternoon of the first Saturday in June, which as any Trentonian can tell you is the first day of the annual Heritage Days festival. The Mill Hill area was teeming with tourists, locals, and old Trentonians from the surrounding townships, some of them quite strange-looking. But surely none of them looked any stranger than the man who was banging on the side of the office of the consulting firm of Werfels and DiTresso.

Lois Werfels, taking her children to visit the bathroom of her husband's office, was startled at the man's appearance. It wasn't only his pallor that struck her, or his ratlike crouch, or the snarling bulldog tattooed on his arm; it was rather all these things together, along with the nice muscles in his legs (he was wearing cutoffs) and his deep-set eyes with their heavy lids and his general air of being the wreck of a very handsome man. Perhaps he had been in prison.

What was he doing pounding on the side of Ernest's office?

Trying to signal someone. Someone inside.

"Children," she said to her three daughters, "I don't think we'll go to the bathroom at Daddy's office this time."

"Whyyy?"

"Oh, Motherrr ..."

"But I have to go potty."

"Stacy, Jessica, Amanda, hush," said Lois Werfels. "We'll use the public rest room at the little theater. That'll be fun. Come this way, girls." As they wheeled about, the hooded eyes followed them. Out of the man's hearing she said to the children, "See if you can see a policeman."

The festival of Heritage Days is a sort of giant street fair celebrating all the ethnic groups that ever settled in Trenton. Every group has a booth, not only the ethnics, but also groups for battered women, runaway children, politicians, druggies, park preservation, and tax revolt. People come from miles around to eat strange food and party.

Needless to say, Nick and Ethel Magaracz were there. The crowd was thick. They saw a lot of people they knew, and a lot more they didn't. Monica Nash bumped right into Magaracz before they recognized each other.

Her curly red hair was down around her shoulders, and she was wearing a checkered sundress. Magaracz noticed she seemed to be freckled all over. She looked nice.

"Mr. Magaracz!" she said with a breathless little laugh. "How nice to see you." She had a paper plate in one hand with a few bites of ethnic food on it. Her other hand was held in the grip of a tall young guy with dark curly hair and a camera. "This is my friend

37

Kevin Mandelbaum," she said. "Kevin, this is Mr. Nicholas Magaracz."

"How do you do, sir," the young guy said, bathing Magaracz in a warm, friendly, almost vacant gaze. "Great day, isn't it? I'm getting some really great pictures."

A Scots pipe band came stamping and booming past. Over the noise Magaracz made introductions. "My wife, Ethel," he said. "Ethel, Monica and Kevin."

"I hope you two are getting something good to eat," Ethel said. "You should try the Bavarian sausage."

"We're vegetarians," said Kevin. "But the *kimchi* is good."

"Did you bring your children?" Magaracz said to Monica.

"They're here somewhere," she said, craning her neck to see over the crowd. "I think they went to watch the belly dancers."

"Hey, belly dancers," said Kevin. "Fantastic. Let's go. Nice meeting you." He plunged off into the crowd, pulling Monica with him. Over the hubbub Magaracz heard Middle Eastern music.

"Who was that?" Ethel asked.

Magaracz said, "That was the woman I was telling you about that I went to see yesterday. You remember. Her husband died and left all this money, only nobody knows what happened to it."

"You never said she was so pretty."

"She's high-strung," Magaracz said. "Very high-strung."

"Is that her son with her?"

Magaracz put his arm around his wife in the old grip, the way they used to go down the halls of Trenton Central High School, fondling her ear with the backs

38

of his knuckles. "No," he murmured in her other ear. "He's her boyfriend."

Ethel said, "Tsk. He's awfully young."

"Not all the women have the good taste to appreciate mature types like me," Magaracz said. "Some of them go for these young guys. Not like you." He pinched her bottom.

"Nick, behave yourself." A contingent of Guardian Angels marched past, fit young blacks and Hispanics in their dashing red berets, unofficial upholders of law and order. A pack of boys ran after them, and from the other direction came a long-haired couple selling ferrets. "Oh, how cute," said Ethel.

"Yeah," Nick said. "Let's go eat."

They shouldered up to the popular Korean stand and got some *kimchi* and a whole pile of other good stuff, with meat in it, and by some lucky chance found a place to sit in the shade. While they were eating, a long line of Japanese ladies in clogs and blue and white kimonos danced by in stately procession, each wagging a small flag in each hand, one flag of Japan and one of the U.S.A. No sooner had they wound out of sight than Howells Gould appeared with his wife, a one-woman entourage, the two of them shaking every available hand.

"Good afternoon, I'm Howells Gould. If you're a resident of Mercer County, I hope you'll vote for me for freeholder."

"Howells," said Magaracz.

"Ah. Nick," Gould said. His proffered hand went fishy, and his eyes slid away in search of more likely votes. The wife smiled frostily.

"You know him?" said Ethel, getting to her feet to watch their royal progress through the crowd.

39

"I know everything about him," Magaracz said. "He knows it, too. Did you see the look he gave me? Which reminds me. I gotta go have a beer with the guys at the Shriners' booth."

"I think I'll go and visit Ruza and Maria Hedervary now," said Ethel, "while you're having your beer with the boys. I promised them I'd stop by the Bosnian booth after lunch."

"After lunch? Why after?"

"Just between you and me, Nick, those Bosnian cabbage dumplings are a little gassy."

As Ethel made her way to the Bosnian booth two policemen pushed past her, jogging away over the bridge across the Assunpink Creek. Something was going on over in the Mill Hill section; a purse-snatching, maybe, Guardian Angels or no.

Ethel found three surly men in possession of the Bosnian booth, and the Hedervary sisters nowhere in sight. "Excuse me," she said to the men, "can you tell me where Ruza and Maria might be?"

"No," one of the men growled. The sausages on the grill were beginning to burn and smoke. The pot with the dumplings in it was boiling over.

"That way," said the young fellow with the nose. She walked in the direction of his pointing finger, and found Ruza sitting under a nearby tree, weeping.

"Why, Ruza," she said, sitting down beside the old lady. "What's wrong?"

"Those horrible men," Ruza said, and blew her nose. "Maria is right. I think we ought to quit the club, too."

"What did they do?"

"They were supposed to come and relieve us at noon," she said, "and they never showed up."

"How inconsiderate."

"Then here they came an hour and a half later, all covered with dirt and sweat and dragging all these notebooks, computer manuals or something, and acting as if they were on some terribly important mission. Who cares about their stupid business, I'd like to know?"

"Computer manuals?" said Ethel. "In a food concession?"

"We waited all that time," Ruza continued, "and my sister almost fainting from the heat of those stoves. She isn't strong, you know. Maria talks tough but she isn't strong. She spoke to them very sharply."

"What excuse did they give?"

"Just nasty words. You should have heard what Herman Eckes said to us. Poor Maria has gone to the ladies' room. They were awful, Eckes and all his horrible friends."

Ethel patted her hand. "There, there, dear," she said.

"They had no right to speak to us that way."

"Of course they didn't."

"Our father founded that club. He knew Herman Eckes's father when he was selling old rags in Goosetown."

"Yes, dear, yes. Don't cry," said Ethel. "It will be all right."

"We used to call him Stinky."

"Of course you did," Ethel murmured. Her friend was wiping her eyes on the apron now, getting streaks of flour on her brow and nose. The two of them got up. "Shall I go see if Maria's all right?" said Ethel.

"No, I'll go," Ruza said. "She might want me, and there's such a crowd in there." She set off toward the

41

little theater, and Ethel walked along with her until they ran into Nick.

"Miss Hedervary!" he said. "I'm glad to see you. I've been meaning to ask you something."

"Ask away," the old lady said.

"You and your sister have been in the Bosnian Club a long time."

She sighed. "Yes, we have. I'm not sure we'll be staying in the club for very much longer."

"Is something funny going on there?"

She said, "Funny? I'd say that would depend on your sense of humor."

"Could it have anything to do with Gilmore Nash?"

Her expression changed to one of complete bewilderment. "Gilmore Nash is dead."

"You spend a lot of time around the clubhouse. Is there any chance he could be still alive, hiding there somewhere?"

"I can't imagine," she said. "What an idea. I'll have to ask Maria what she thinks about it. Excuse me." She went away into the crowd.

"Ruza is very upset," Ethel said.

"Sorry to hear that," he said. "Say, guess what. Some junkies broke into Werfels and DiTresso's office just now and tore it all up."

Ethel sighed. "Every time I go out with you something terrible happens."

SIX

ON MONDAY MORNING Magaracz considered the problem of motorcyclists following him, and then dismissed it, since nobody had been behind him on the way in today. Then he reconsidered the parking permit.

Against the promptings of his better nature he had kept Badger's parking permit, and found it an enormous convenience. It was made to be a window sticker, but Badger had put it between two pieces of transparent plastic so as to be able to move it from one car to another and tuck it in the edge of the window. For Magaracz the alternatives to parking in Area Six were disagreeable. He could drive halfway out of town on State Street, leave the car on a side street, and hike back into town; he could risk his battery and hubcaps on Hanover Street; or he could pay an arm and a leg to one of the lots over there and maybe still lose his battery and hubcaps.

He knew that honor demanded that he give the permit back to the State. But still. It was really Badger's, right? He earned it through long State service. And, of course, Badger couldn't use it anymore. What Magaracz must do then, was to earn it somehow, maybe by checking out Badger's suspicious death. It was al-

43

most like Badger was a client. And the parking sticker was Magaracz's fee. Having salved his conscience once again on this matter, Magaracz picked up the phone, which had started to ring.

It was Roger Diefnagel. "I have some mail here addressed to Os Badger," he said. "It's in response to a letter that he seems to have sent out in a mass mailing."

"To everybody on my list?" said Magaracz.

"Yes, but not all of them replied. Our people are going to handle the ones who wrote, if they seem straightforward, and you can continue to check the others. Out of the original thirty-two we have heard from twenty-five. Some of the replies don't look quite right to me, and I'd like you to check them out. Just the same, you ought to see a big decrease in your workload."

Oswald Badger and his secretary had done the mailing on the new word processor, as a sort of experiment. "I think he would have been pleased with the results," Diefnagel said wistfully.

"Tell me something," said Magaracz. "Are there any replies from a Monica Nash?"

There weren't.

"Okay," said Magaracz. Certainly she hadn't mentioned a letter; she seemed completely surprised to have him turn up on her doorstep, as if she'd never heard of any inheritance before. "What was in the letter they sent out?"

"I'll send you a copy," Diefnagel said, "along with the questionable replies."

"I'd appreciate it," said Magaracz.

So Lora turned up to deliver the whole works, piled

44

in a small cardboard box she had found in Oswald Badger's old office.

When Magaracz had sorted it all out he found two half-empty packs of breath mints at the bottom of the box, a catalogue from Abe's War Surplus, and a copy of *Modern Warrior* magazine. Oswald Badger's name was on the catalogue; it seemed to have been mailed to him at home.

Some of the items in the catalogue were circled.

Magaracz was greatly intrigued with the thought of Oswald Badger, with his paunch and balding head, owning and reading this war surplus catalogue. And selecting items from it. Camouflage jumpsuits. Khaki underwear. Combat boots, size eight. Small feet. And reading *Modern Warrior*, which was a periodical for would-be mercenaries and guys with soldier complexes. Here was an ad in the personals, which somebody had marked with a yellow highlighter:

REACH FOR REAL MANHOOD

Sick of working for the Taxocracy? The free life you dream of can be yours. Send resume with $5 application fee to MW Box 13230. Principals only.

What was the story with Badger? What was this stuff? A double life? A secret fantasy existence as a mercenary? Was he reaching too hard for real manhood, when he cashed in his chips? Or what? And why did he throw away his pants?

I wonder, Magaracz said to himself, and he made up a fake résumé and put it in an envelope with a check for five dollars.

*　　*　　*

A shaft of sunlight struggled through green burlap curtains and cast an unhealthy light over the broad, low-ceilinged attic of the Bosnian-American Social Club. It was a large room, filled with things, not in the abandoned way of most attics but rather in a way that suggested constant use.

Cabinets lined the walls, and a fair-sized bookcase that held many books. The complete works of Ayn Rand were there, along with J. Edgar Hoover's *Masters of Deceit, The Prince* by Niccolò Machiavelli, *Mein Kampf*, and *The Protocols of the Learned Elders of Zion*. Periodicals were stacked there too, rightwing newspapers, handgun magazines, *Modern Warrior*.

Two Doberman pinschers were stretched out on the floor with their front paws crossed, drowsing, and some layers of newspaper in the corner bore evidence of animal ordure.

But the Bosnians used their attic for more than a library and dog kennel. There were work tables, fitted up for different activities. On one table were rolls of different thicknesses of electrical wire, wire cutters, packages of something that might have been gray modeling clay, but wasn't, batteries of all sizes, a digital clock, a black plastic casing about half the size of a shoebox, with no works in it, and some bits of electronic equipment.

A second table bore a small photocopying machine, five reams of paper, wrapped, a box of 9 x 12 catalogue envelopes, an Addressograph machine, and a pile of stapled newsletters waiting to be mailed to the members and supporters of the local branch of the Posse

46

Comitatus. On the third table was a home computer with disk drive and printer, various software manuals, a spiral-bound notebook, a plastic rack stuffed with floppy disks, some felt-tip pens, pencils, graph paper, and a pocket calculator.

Four men were gathered around the green face of the computer screen.

"Okay," said Dr. Eckes, "now that you've hooked it up, what is it?"

"This is a modem," Ace Jeder said. "With this little item I can call up the State's computer, and our computer can talk to it."

"What does our computer plan to say?" asked Bill Sherbrook, scratching his ear.

"Well, according to Rory," said the Ace, "computer tapes are the basis for most of the State's operations."

"Okay," the doctor said.

"If that's true," the Ace said, "then all we have to do is tell their computer to erase the tapes. A neat little piece of citizen action. No bloodshed, no violence, just — pow! — and the State of New Jersey is functionally disabled. We won't even have to use the guns and explosives, or anyway not before the Russians come."

"How do we do it?" the doctor said.

"I've been studying these specs we stole from Werfels and DiTresso," said the Ace. "Their security is based on one software package that manages all the tapes, keeps track of the tape numbers, when the tapes were created, and when they're supposed to expire."

"So . . ."

"So we'll dial up their computer and tell their tape management system that all their tapes have expired."

"Will it believe you?" said Nash, raising his eyebrows.

"Why not? I have a valid log-on code. Their system will then release all the tapes that they told it to save. By the end of the week, other applications will have erased the data on their old tapes by writing over it."

"I thought Rory told us that they keep copies at some remote site, in case of fire or disaster."

"Oh, they do. But that's the beauty of their security package. If a tape is defined to the system as a scratch tape, the program prints out a list of scratch tape numbers on a report. Then somebody drives out to the remote site, collects all the tapes whose numbers appear on the list, and brings them back to the main computer room to be written on. It's what they always do. No need for mere humans to question it."

"So then, by the end of next week . . . ," mused the doctor.

"No more salaries for bureaucrats," the Ace said.

"No welfare checks."

"No licenses to operate beauty parlors."

"No pensions for retired judges."

"No state income tax."

"No reports for the legislature on the intimate details of our private lives."

"No permits to remove asbestos."

"No funds for repressive highway signs."

"No paychecks for the State Police."

Something about the scene reminded Gilmore Nash of savages around a campfire. He himself was thinking even at that moment that nonviolent means were seldom effective. He was making his own plans to disable the State. When the others failed he meant to be ready.

Nash made a soft clicking noise with his mouth, and the two Dobermans stood up.

"I'm going," he said. "See you guys later."

"Don't get into trouble," said Eckes. "We don't want any more screwups."

Nash stopped. "What do you mean, more screwups?"

The dogs growled.

"It seems," said Eckes, "we have a tax man coming around because of your messing with the arms money, Gil. At about the time that Batt was supposed to be cremating you."

"So what's the problem?" said Nash. "Can't you guys handle him?"

"We'll handle him," said Dr. Eckes. "We handled the other ones. But it makes more trouble for us at a time when we should be directing our energies toward other things. What I'm saying is, no unnecessary trouble right now."

"What other ones?" said Sherbrook. There was a frantic round of eye contact. Nash glared at the doctor, the doctor squinted at the Ace, who stared at his knuckles, and Sherbrook gazed into their faces one after another. Nobody answered him. The doctor cleared his throat.

"Trouble?" said Nash. "What sort of trouble did you have in mind?"

"Oh, say, like somebody seeing you who knows you," said Eckes. "Or like the police picking you up for some reason."

49

"Nobody will see me. I walk in the woods, or I ride my bicycle, for which I need no license or identification. Anyone who knew me wouldn't recognize me anyway with the bicycle helmet on, and Monica is the only person on the East Coast who ever saw me in a full beard." They all looked at him in silence.

"I'm not about to expose myself to Monica, if that's what's on your mind," he said. He might have added that he wasn't half as conspicuous as Dwayne and the other make-believe soldiers, due back any day now from funny camp in Illinois. Sergeant Rock and Easy Company. If they didn't shoot off their feet out there.

"Don't worry about it, then," said Eckes. "No problem."

Nash grunted and went down the stairs. The dogs went after him. The kitchen door banged.

"Where's he going?" said Sherbrook.

"Home to do his laundry," said the doctor.

"Home?" said Sherbrook. "You mean where he used to live?"

"He does it once a week," said the doctor. "Don't tell me you didn't know that."

"Won't his wife notice?"

"What would she notice?" said the doctor. "A little missing soap powder, a slight rise in the gas bill. His wife doesn't notice things like that. She's crazy anyway. A certifiable lunatic. No one would believe anything she said. She never came to his funeral. Did you know that?" Sherbrook shook his head, and scratched his ear again.

"There," the Ace said, as he typed in a final command. "That should do it. By this time next week the

50

government of the State of New Jersey will be history."

"Good," said the doctor. "We'll sit back and let it happen. As far as Nicholas Magaracz is concerned, as soon as the others get back from the training camp, you and Dwayne can take care of him."

The Ace snickered. "Dwayne can give him what he gave that soldier at Fort Dix."

"What soldier?" said Sherbrook.

SEVEN

GILMORE NASH had once invested a good deal of money in his mattress, which exactly suited the needs of his back. He saw no reason to forgo its pleasures merely because he was supposed to be dead.

What he would do on washday was to cycle through the woods to his old home and let himself in through the basement door, leaving his dogs in the bushes along with his ten-speed and bicycle helmet. In the basement he would remove his clothes and put them in the washer-dryer, together with the dirty laundry in his backpack. Then up to his old bed for a luxurious nap, followed by a shower, after which he would collect his clothes, dogs, and bicycle and return to the Bosnian Club. Sometimes he went into his sons' room and thought about how he would take them away and they would all go back out west.

Waking up in time to get out before his wife came home was never a problem for Gilmore Nash. Combat-hardened, he slept like an animal, always on the edge of wakefulness. He could say to himself, "I'll get up at three fifteen," and some internal clock would snap him to attention.

But he was getting older.

On the afternoon in question, he slept straight on through.

The sound of Monica coming in the front door with someone else, talking, woke him. Faster than thought he rolled out of the bed and into the linen closet, which had a space under the first shelf big enough for a man to curl up in.

Once he was in the linen closet, though, Nash was completely at a loss. There was no way to get out unobserved. The bedroom door could be seen from everywhere in the house; the bedroom window was blocked with a heavy air conditioner. He drew his knees up under his chin, reflecting sourly that now he no longer lived here the linen closet seemed to be stuffed with sweet-smelling towels and sheets.

That wasn't the way he remembered it. Monica, he always thought, went out of her way to make sure the towels got moldy, and little Henry peed the bed no matter how Nash beat him and of course had to have new sheets almost every morning. As for their own bed, Monica didn't fool with the sheets much, not to change them or wash them or anything. Not like his mother.

"There's a smell in the bedclothes, Kevin," said Monica, coming into the room. "In here is where the atmosphere is the strongest. I want these vibrations working on the reading."

"We'll set up the card table over here, then, and light a couple of candles." A man's voice. "If there's anything, we should pick it up. Although I'm not really sure that a Tarot reading is the right way to do it. It seems to me that the Ouija board . . ."

"Oh, God, no, Kevin, not that. What if I started getting messages from him? I didn't want to hear from

53

him when he was alive. You don't know what he was like."

"But then, what . . ."

"All I want from this is an answer to my question," she said. There were sounds of a card table being set up.

The man said, "You washed your hands, didn't you? It's important, before we start."

"Yes, dear," she said. The light under the linen closet door grew fainter and then came up again, flickering. Far away a cricket chirped.

"Do you want to tell me what your question is?"

"Yes," she said. "Yes. My question is this. Will I ever be rid of Gilmore in my heart?"

"Poor Monica," the man said. "Does his death still bother you so much?"

"Not his death," she said. "It's like I was telling you, I feel . . . I sense his presence sometimes. It's ugly, Kevin. You understand, don't you? I'm . . . affected by it."

"You mean your headaches," Kevin said.

"Yes. Maybe." The sound of a match striking a folder, another flicker of light, a whiff of cigarette smoke. A sigh. "I want to have a free and happy life."

"You think Gilmore is somehow haunting you."

"Haunting me. Yes. It would be just like him."

"Okay," said Kevin. "We'll just go with that. Think about being free, and take these cards and shuffle them. Any way you want to."

Riffling cards. The deck being tapped on the table. "Concentrate on your question," said Kevin. "Think about being free." His voice was droning, as if he had said these words many times. "Now cut the cards in three piles, left to right. . . ."

Card sounds. Nash could almost hear their breath, the breath that must have been causing the candles to flicker, casting irregular light through the crack under the closet door.

"I think the Queen of Cups should be your significator," said Kevin. "Fair-haired, poetic, and imaginative. This covers you." The faint slap of a card. "This crosses you." Slap. "The foundation of the matter . . . Passing away . . . Possibility . . . Certain to come."

"Are those all the cards you use, the ones in the cross?"

"Concentrate on your question," said Kevin. "Four more cards. Your fears. What your friends think. Your hopes. The final outcome."

Each of these pronouncements was followed by the slap of a card. Then there was silence.

"Oh, heavens," said Monica.

"Now, remember, Monica, it isn't as bad as you might think," said Kevin. "Often the cards are simply pointing the way to a path of greater spiritual fulfillment."

"But, death, Kevin? Death covers me? How can that be spiritually fulfilling?" She was whining.

Kevin talked to her in a soothing voice. "The Death card never means death," he said. "It means change, rebirth, renewal. It means a great change in your way of life."

"You're sure?" she said. "Even upside down like this?"

"Death, reversed . . . Let me look it up. I don't think I've ever done a reading with Death reversed in it."

Monica whimpered. Pages made a sound of turning. "It could mean a number of things," said Kevin. "Death of a political figure, or political upheaval of some sort, possibly revolution. Not your death, my dear. Perhaps it's a warning to stay out of politics."

"I haven't been political since the war ended," she said. "But these other cards. They're all swords."

"Yes," he said. "The nine of swords crosses you. Misery, suffering, dishonesty, lies . . ."

"But what does it mean?" she said.

"We'll have to look at it in context. The foundation of the matter is the three of swords. Sorrow, separation of lovers, possibly civil strife and upheaval . . ."

"It doesn't make any sense to me," said Monica. "Although I suppose Gilmore and I were lovers once."

"Eight of swords, behind you and passing away. Bondage, imprisonment, betrayal . . . But, as you see, passing away. I think the outlook is good for your free and happy life."

"And the next card?"

"This represents a possible future. The five of swords. It could mean conquest of others by unfair means, or it might signify some physical threat. . . ."

"It looks grim to me, Kevin." she said. "Gilmore is written all over my reading."

"For the immediate future, that which is before you . . . The King of Swords, reversed. Could be a man with dark brown hair and brown eyes, cruel and malicious."

"Gilmore! That's Gilmore," she said. "In my future? Then it's true, isn't it; he's haunting this house."

"Sh, sh," he said. "You're getting overexcited. Be calm. This is supposed to be a calm process, this reading. There. There. You're trembling."

"I'm sorry, darling," she said.

56

"Mellow out. Think of a beach, with the tide slowly coming in. Drink this."

"Thank you."

"Your husband must have been a very forceful person to have such a strong effect on you," he said. "I almost wish I could have known him, if only so that I could understand you better."

She laughed. "You wouldn't want to know Gilmore," she said. "For one thing he was a howling anti-Semite."

"Really?" he said.

"I always thought it was those newsletters he got. As far as I know, he never saw a real Jew until we came east, except maybe somebody he knew in the Marines. But he had all these weird ideas about what they were up to, and how they were conspiring against him and stuff."

"Was he sane otherwise?"

"I don't really know," she said. "What's the Moon?"

"The moon?"

"The next card. The Moon. You said it was my fears."

"Oh, yes. Right. Your fears. Sleep and dreams, secret foes, nightmares maybe. You are very fearful about the outcome of this matter, very much disturbed about it. As for your friends and family, their view is expressed here by the four of swords, which means . . ." Sound of pages turning. "A rest from anxiety, release from suffering."

"It looks to me like a dead man," she said.

"No, no," he said. "Definitely not a card of death. A card of rest. Repose. That's what the people who love you see you having. We all do."

Her voice was low. "All those swords."

"Well, here," he said heartily. "Here's a card that isn't a sword. The Star. Excellent card. Good health. Great love. Radiant cosmic energy. The position of the card signifies that it has to do with your hopes, I might point out."

"It's upside down."

"Hm. Well, reversed, the Star has other meanings."

"Such as?"

"Pessimism . . . Mental illness . . ."

"Some hopes," she said.

"You know, Monica," he said, "I don't think this is a true reading we're getting here. All this political upheaval and strife. It doesn't seem to have any bearing on the question you asked. Maybe we should just call it a night, and try for a better reading tomorrow."

"There's only one card you haven't read, though. Don't you think we should finish?"

He said, "It just seems to me . . ."

"Come on, Kevin."

He took an audible breath. "Okay. This card stands for the final outcome. As you can see, it's the Tower."

She said, "I suppose you're going to tell me that this isn't a card of death either, with the fire coming out of the top, and those people falling."

He said, "Not a card of death. It has more to do with the casting down of material existence on the way to enlightenment. In fact, you know, that's mainly what Tarot is all about. It's an aid to meditation, for spiritual growth."

There was a long period of silence. The two seemed to have come to some failure of mutual expectations. Gilmore tried to move his left foot and was enraged to discover that it was asleep; electric needles stabbed him.

At last Monica said, "I don't know why I should think of it, but did you know that Gilmore was a demolition expert in Vietnam?"

Kevin said, "What was he, Special Forces?"

"Marine Reconnaissance Battalion."

"Those guys were tough," he said. "He must have been really tough."

She sighed. "He was tough all right. I don't want to think about him anymore."

"Okay, let's leave this," he said. "Take off your clothes and lie on the bed, and I'll rub your back."

"Wait, Kevin, let me change the sheets!"

"No," said Kevin. It was just as well, because Nash would have killed them both if they had opened the door to the closet, first him, and then her, no matter what Dr. Eckes had to say about it. Well, that could wait. He would come back for them after the big job was done. In the ensuing total social and economic collapse no one would notice a couple of bodies more or less. Then he could take his boys out west, and bring them up there as real men. None of this gypsy garbage.

The flickering light under his door went out. As the soft moos and sighs of the back rub gave way to giggles and sounds of bedsprings bouncing, Nash began to be really bothered by the state of his feet and legs. If he didn't stand up soon they would be paralyzed.

I'll give her a haunting, anyway, he thought. Silently he pushed the door open and got to his numb feet. After a moment he stepped to the foot of the bed, stark naked as he was, into a patch of moonlight.

The effect on Monica was better than he could have dreamed. As soon as she saw him she burst into loud incoherent shrieks of hysteria. He stepped back out of

59

the light and went to get his clothes, before the Jew boyfriend could roll over and see him, and know that he was real after all. There would be time for that.

Monica was still screaming. *Woo! Wah!* The noise of it followed him deep into the woods as he pedaled along the path back to the club, his dogs running along behind him.

Herman Eckes was in the Bosnian Club's comfort station when he heard the wheels of Gilmore Nash's bicycle swishing past in the darkness, followed by the panting noises of the dogs. *Enough for now,* he thought, and began packing up his recording equipment. He had been working on a tape explaining his political beliefs. It was Eckes's plan to play this tape over the radio when the destruction of the government was complete, so that the citizens would know who to thank and why the deed had been done.

He had carried the tape recorder into the comfort station because the liveness of the cinder-block walls and concrete floor gave a wonderful quality to his voice. When he played it back it sounded to him as though he were addressing a huge crowd in an amphitheater.

The beliefs of Herman Eckes were actually few and very simple. He believed:

1. The Russians were coming.
2. The people were too degenerate to care.
3. It was the government's fault.
4. Those who knew must save the country.

He was very pleased with the tape. He had been at it off and on for a week or so, and with a little bit more work it would be ready to go. He would send it to the news department of some radio station. Maybe he would make copies first.

Should he take it inside to play it for Gilmore Nash? Everyone else was asleep.

But, no. Some instinct told the doctor that Nash's political sentiments were not really the same as his own, that his politics were in fact tainted with self-interest in ways that Eckes didn't want to hear about. There were things that Nash was more interested in than justice and the American way. A glaze came over his eyes when the doctor spoke of the government, an expression that Eckes never saw on the faces of the others. The others revered him. Gilmore Nash . . .

Here was the thing, and Herman Eckes didn't want to face it: Gilmore Nash was with them for some purpose other than to uphold the truth. Once Eckes was forced to acknowledge this, Nash would have to be cast out. But the group needed him. He was the only one with real military experience.

So Dr. Eckes passed up the chance to play his tape for Gilmore Nash, and instead played it for himself twice more. He liked it a lot. The birds were beginning their first warbles of dawn as the last meaty phrase rang out again:

"Restore this land of our forefathers to its true state of freedom!"

Dr. Eckes smiled, and went in to bed.

EIGHT

MONICA NASH regarded the heaping plateful of breakfast in front of her with dull eyes.

"Darling, won't you eat something?" said Kevin.

"Maybe after a while."

"These eggs won't be any good after a while," he said. He was worried. Monica's inexplicable screaming fit of the night before had raised a frightening question in his mind.

What if Monica was as crazy as they said?

The headaches, the memory lapses, the wild accusations against her dead husband, and now this. Perhaps if she were to see someone professionally. "Do you want to talk to Jonathan?" he said to her.

She blinked at him. Jonathan was a colleague of his in psychiatric social work who was known for his success in treating mad housewives.

"If you think I should talk to Jonathan," she said, "okay."

Russ Woodshard trundled the last weary hand-truckload of computer tapes out to Data Processing's delivery van. Every Tuesday they sent him to the re-

62

mote site to pick up expired tapes, and every Tuesday he did his job without complaining, but he had never seen anything like this.

Driving back, he debated whether he should speak to his supervisor, Howard Ucksby, about it. On the one hand, thought Woodshard, the volume of scratch tapes was so unusually large that it might signal something wrong in the system. On the other hand, Ucksby was such a complete dickhead that he would probably just give him a hard time.

Woodshard rehearsed a couple of different approaches, but when he got back to the shop he forgot them. Ucksby was yelling at another operator for bringing a lighted cigarette into the computer room.

It was Ucksby's standard rant, newly embellished, which he delivered at the top of his voice whenever he so much as suspected that one of his operators might be considering creating heat or smoke in the neighborhood of the new Halon alarm system. This system, installed at enormous expense, was designed to protect the delicate computer equipment from threat of fire. In case it detected heat or smoke the system was to ring a loud bell and discharge a special gas, guaranteed to smother all flames and slow-footed operators. To smoke in the presence of the Halon system would be to force the evacuation of the computer room and the untimely shutdown of the computers. On top of this inconvenience and expense would be the cost of recharging the gas, many thousands of dollars.

The very thought of such a possibility was enough to drive Howard Ucksby to amazing flights of profanity. His outburst was stupefying, even when not delivered at oneself, and it drove everything he had meant to say out of Russ Woodshard's mind. Rob Fenkis, the offending smoker, slunk away. Woodshard stepped up and blurted out his message.

"There were too many tapes this week, Howard."

"What do you mean?" Ucksby said. "What's the problem?"

"There were twenty times as many tapes as usual. That's an awful lot of tapes. It just seems like too many."

"Aw, are they too heavy for poor little you? What's the matter, numb nuts, you afraid of a little work?"

Roger Diefnagel called Magaracz to set up a meeting. Marcia Hoover wanted to discuss certain data processing ramifications of the death tape job. "We'll meet at ten in Os Badger's old office," he said. "There's a conference table. We'll be more comfortable."

Badger's office was indeed comfortable, although stripped of his personal effects it had a forlorn air. The desk was bare, and there were light-colored square marks on the wall, with nails and hooks where pictures or certificates had hung. The floor had a rug on it. It was nothing like Magaracz's cramped cube.

Maybe he ought to try for a promotion.

Marcia was on time as usual, loaded with brown envelopes and pads of paper. Diefnagel introduced her to Magaracz. She put her things down.

"I have bad news for you," she said.

They waited while she collected her thoughts.

"There's something strange going on with the tape master files for the Inheritance Tax system."

"Yes?" Diefnagel prompted.

"Nobody will own up, but my bank tapes got mysteriously scratched. I won't be able to rerun the death tape job."

"I don't understand. Why not?" Diefnagel said.

"Because the bank tape was — actually there are seven tape reels in the bank tape file. One of the reels was written over last night, in effect destroying the file. I can't get anybody to tell me how it happened." She seemed upset. "Either there's a bug in the tape management system, or somebody is out to get me. Or the Inheritance Tax system."

"Or the State," Magaracz offered. "Lots of people are out to get the State. Don't take it personally." She seemed to cheer up a little.

"Has anyone else had a problem?" Diefnagel said.

"Good question," she said. "I'll have to ask around."

"What about the death tape?" said Magaracz.

"Oh," she said, "that's fine. That isn't an in-house tape. Human Services produced it in their shop, so it was never catalogued in our tape management system, and we don't keep it downstairs with the other tapes. It's under my chair, in fact. Why?"

"I wonder if you could find out something for me," said Magaracz. "Can you check on the names of all the people on the death tape whose death certificates were signed by a Dr. Herman Eckes?"

"You're talking data base. We don't have this stuff on data base."

"Isn't there any way to get at it?"

She thought it over for a minute. "Maybe a little utility run . . . We could charge it to user assistance and do it as a test, so the auditors wouldn't notice. Print out all the records that have Eckes's name in the physician field. I could do it right now, but it wouldn't be formatted. You'd have to pick out the names of your dead people from a lot of letters and numbers all run together."

"I could handle that," said Magaracz. "I'm a detective. You know?"

She smiled. "I'll do it as soon as I get back," she said.

As Russ Woodshard rolled the last load of tapes up the ramp to the computer room door, two men came up behind him, talking in low voices.

"Very state-of-the-art," one was saying, "considering how little was budgeted for security." Woodshard glanced over his shoulder. Two guys in dark suits and ties were taking a tour of the place.

Woodshard stuck his foot under one wheel of the truck to keep it from rolling back, and fished in his pockets for his key card. Who were those guys? They looked familiar.

"You feel that the security could be better," said the one with the curly hair.

"Anything could be *better*," said the bald-headed one, groveling a little. Oh, right, that was Ernest Werfels, the consultant. "Anything could be better with more *money*. But it's *good*. Very good."

Woodshard found his key card and stuck it in the slot.

"For instance, look at this," said Werfels.

"What of it?" said the other man.

"You see that nobody can even get into the computer room without a special key card."

"What is he taking in there?"

"As you see, tapes."

"What tapes?"

"Excuse me, son," said Werfels. "What tapes are those?"

The State Treasurer, that's who that dude was. Woodshard had seen his picture in the paper one time. He was the biggest mahoff in the place. "Uh, scratch tapes," Woodshard said.

The computer room door swung in on a deafening racket; all the printers were clacking and buzzing, the disk drives were clunking, the tape drives were whirring, the consoles beeping, everything making maximum noise. The two men followed him into the din.

Howard Ucksby popped up from behind a tape drive like a troll from behind a toadstool and began to move toward them menacingly.

The Treasurer was picking up the tapes on the hand truck and reading the labels.

"Retired judges master file," he said.

"What?" said Werfels.

"This label says that New Jersey's retired judges are all on this tape. The Pensions System. Won't they need this tape to pay the judges their pensions?"

"I can't hear you."

"Who let you in here?" Ucksby bellowed. "Nobody gets in here without a key card or a pass."

"Retired judges," mused the Treasurer, "are very powerful men and women."

"Ernest Werfels, Mr. Ucksby; you remember me. I did some consulting work here last year. And of course you know Mr. Golfin."

"Golfin?" said Ucksby.

"The State Treasurer," Werfels explained.

"Oh. Right," said Ucksby. Of course, he didn't know the Treasurer, even though ultimately the Treasurer was his boss; cabinet officers came and went, but the lower depths of the bureaucracy went on forever. Confused and embarrassed, Ucksby barked at Russ Woodshard: "Get those tapes out of here."

"Just a minute," the Treasurer said. "I want to look at some more of those scratch tapes. A scratch tape is a tape that can be written over, is that right?"

"Those are all expired," said Ucksby. "They've been sent back from remote storage."

"You don't keep them very long," the Treasurer observed. "This one was created last Friday, it says here."

"Oh," said Werfels, "there must be some mistake."

They were all shouting to make themselves heard. Woodshard stood patiently, balancing the hand truck, while the Treasurer pulled more tapes off the pile.

"Created yesterday . . . Created last week . . . File of division heads and cabinet officers, Payroll System . . . Tell me," he shouted at Russ, "is this an unusual number of scratch tapes?"

"Yeah," Russ replied. "I said something about it to Mr. Ucksby, but he didn't seem to think it was important. This is the third truckload."

"Where are the other two truckloads?" the Treasurer demanded.

"Back in the tape library. Probably filed away already."

Scowling, the Treasurer took Howard Ucksby by the elbow and led him back out of sight among the tape drives. Russ Woodshard and Ernest Werfels waited, avoiding each other's eyes. All over the computer room operators were peering furtively around the machines, wondering what was up.

Suddenly the print jobs that were running all ended at once, and the printers fell silent. The Treasurer's voice rang out very clearly.

"See about it," he said. "Whatever it takes, check it out. I don't know whether you can imagine what will happen if those judges don't get paid. If you can't, then try to imagine what will happen if I don't get paid. To start with, you won't get paid. Do I make myself clear?"

"Yeah," said Ucksby. "Clear." They came out from behind the tape drives; Ucksby was sweating visibly. Russ Woodshard did not jeer and laugh at him, but with a serious expression, stared intently at the upper northeast corner of the room and softly hummed the chorus of an old tune by The Doors.

Marcia brought Magaracz another printout. "Here's a record layout of this output for you. I told you it would be hard to read. Some of the numbers are in packed format, so you have to . . ."

"Honey," he said, "I can't make heads or tails of this garbage."

"You'd like me to run another little test, and format the output, right?"

"Please."

"I thought you might. The fact is I stripped off all the records that have Eckes's name in the physician field to a test file on disk, so they won't have to fool with any more tapes down there. I'm getting kind of interested in this guy myself. The number of folks who died under his care is, to say the least, disproportionate."

"Disproportionate to what?" said Magaracz.

"To the number of other doctors whose patients

died. There are a couple of guys in inner city hospital emergency rooms who signed almost as many death certificates as your friend here, but he holds the record."

"No kidding."

"What do you want to know about his victims? I mean, patients?" she said.

"I'm not sure. What's to know?"

"The records carry age, sex, date of death, who handled the funeral, the name of the next of kin who signed off on the body —"

"Yeah. Yeah. All that stuff," he said.

"Want it sorted any special way? I can throw in a utility sort for good measure."

"Good. Sort it . . . sort it by zip code," said Magaracz, thinking that would make it easier to do follow-up legwork if it looked like being useful.

Meanwhile the Ace was lunching with his friend Rory.

"It's the strangest thing," said Rory. "They found out that whoever did it used my log-on code and password. I thought it must have been one of the guys looking over my shoulder when I signed on. It's a terrible feeling, knowing that somebody is out to get you that way."

"Probably one of the straights," said the Ace. "They can be so bitchy."

"But then after the Treasurer left, the chief of operations came and told Ucksby the Governor had called saying he got a tip from the FBI that someone was sabotaging the tapes. Go figure it. The FBI."

"Weird," the Ace said. Was there a mole in their midst? He must discuss it with the doctor.

70

They ate their patty melts in silence for a while.

"Who could it have been?" said Rory. "Unless it was one of the systems programmers; they can look all the passwords up. I never told anybody my password, except . . . except you, Ace. . . ." He began to toy with the stirrer in his Long Island iced tea, staring at it intently.

"Tell me something," he said at last. "Why did you use to ask me all that stuff?"

The Ace composed his features into a smile of friendliness. "I was just making conversation, Rory," he said. "Passing the time."

"Really. You know, though, it's a funny coincidence that it was my log-on code that was used to get on and trash the tape management system."

"I must agree," said the Ace. "I can't understand it at all. Unless, as you said, some systems programmer had it in for you."

"Ace, I'm going to lose my job over this. Have you any idea how bad things have to be before they fire somebody from the State?"

"You told me you didn't like your job," the Ace said.

Rory examined his food as though he had found a half-eaten roach in it. He was not at all happy. *What does he want from me?* thought the Ace. *Apologies? A full confession?*

"I don't like to be used by people I thought were my friends, you know," Rory said to him. "In fact, I hate it."

"It's not what you think, Rory." The Ace patted his hand.

"Yes, it is. It's exactly what I think." He crumpled his napkin, and flung it onto the table, and got up and left. It was the last Ace Jeder ever saw of him.

The Ace went back to the club and reported that his plan to bring Taxation to its knees had failed. "They know something's going on," he said. "They're cleaning it up. They've changed all the log-on codes, so I can't get in anymore, and I've lost my inside contact."

Gilmore Nash and Dr. Eckes were eating their lunch of chili dogs and beer at the kitchen table when the Ace announced this news. The doctor said, "Pity. The rest of the men are due back tomorrow morning."

Nash said, "It doesn't matter."

"What do you mean?" said the Ace. "The plan has failed."

"Only if we let it. You say this guy told you it would take them days to sort out the tapes and put them back in order."

"Yes, but —"

"Meanwhile they're all in the computer room, the off-site tapes and everything."

"Right, but they aren't —"

"We destroy the building," said Gilmore Nash.

"But —"

"Destroy the building, destroy the tapes. That will be the end of the State of New Jersey's tax gathering capabilities for years to come. Not only the tapes, but all their equipment . . ."

"Yes."

"Their personnel."

A long silence while they thought over the implications of this.

"That's murder," the Ace said.

"Not the first, though, is it?" said Nash. "Not even the second, I think."

Was he sneering? The doctor gave him an embarrassed look. The first incident he spoke of, greatly to be regretted, had happened to Dwayne Murchison and his men when they were on maneuvers.

In the old days, maneuvers used to involve something very different from getting on a train and going to southern Illinois to run through a pile of tires with a bunch of midwestern survivalists. In the old days Dr. Eckes's followers had their own place to go on maneuvers, before they were cast out as from the Garden of Eden. It had happened the previous summer.

They were camped in a shell hole on the target range at Fort Dix, in the heart of the Pine Barrens. The location had kept the local pineys, who usually knew everything that went on, from finding them out. None of the locals ever went there for fear of being killed by Army gunfire.

But Dwayne Murchison and the others considered that their already dead status gave them charmed lives. And indeed, they had no trouble except for the night that the soldier found them sleeping.

The first they heard of him was the noise he made tripping over their beer bottles. One of the LFD woke up and cursed at him. Luckily Dwayne was sleeping in another shell hole, so that when the soldier started poking them and giving them a hard time he was able to come up behind him and put a bayonet where it would do the most good.

According to the newspapers the next day, the authorities thought one of the soldier's friends must have done it in a gambling fight or some such thing. Still, after that they could never go there anymore. It was the secret shame of the LFD.

The doctor cleared his throat. "I think you'll agree,

73

though, Gil, that we would have to leave the area if we were to do such a thing."

"Probably true, doc," said Gilmore. "Maybe it's time for us to split up anyhow, you know? Carry the message to different parts of the country. Stuff like that." The doctor looked at him oddly, suspecting him again of faking his ideological convictions. As of course he was. What Gilmore Nash wanted was to blow things up.

The doctor took a deep breath. "Very well. Let us all make our plans, and then we'll take out the Tax building. As a matter of fact I've had a very attractive offer for this place from the New Zinderneuf Trap Rock Company. Now it's my turn to start a new life."

"Where will you go?" said Ace Jeder.

The doctor smiled. "Argentina sounds like a good place, don't you think?"

"Why Argentina?"

"Oh, I don't know," said the doctor. "I could buy a few cows, start a ranch. . . ."

"Where are you going to go, Gil?" said the Ace.

"Do you have a need to know?" said Nash.

"Will you go back to your wife?" he asked.

Back to my wife, thought Gilmore Nash, and the idea seemed to burn into his brain like an ash he had dropped on a sofa once, a tiny hole, a little smell of smoke, and after a long time it caught fire.

"We can think about the plans we have to make," the doctor said. "We'll have a meeting when the others get back from camp, and decide just what's to be done. I do think that now it's particularly important for that tax man not to give us any trouble. Ace, I want you to get on him again."

"Right," said the Ace.

*   *   *

It was a fine summer afternoon, and there were other people on Magaracz's list besides Gilmore Nash. He decided to drive up to Bergenfield to check out the heirs of one Matthew Toddhunter.

All the way up the Garden State Parkway he thought he saw the kid from the Bosnian Club following him, now behind him, now in front, his monumental nose hidden under a round motorcycle helmet that caused him to look less like a bird and more like a huge grasshopper. Magaracz knew him just the same, by his shoulder blades, and by his red hands with their knobby knuckles. When Magaracz got off at the Bergenfield exit the kid did not follow quite so closely, and when he turned down the quiet, tree-lined street where the Toddhunters lived, the kid and his motorcycle were nowhere in sight.

A soft chime sounded somewhere inside the big stone house when Magaracz pressed the doorbell. A uniformed maid opened the solid oak door. Mrs. Toddhunter, she told him, was lying down; Mr. Toddhunter wasn't home; he should come back another time. Over her shoulder Magaracz glimpsed the trappings of the quietly moneyed life, soft rugs, a dignified grandfather clock, real oil paintings of unreal green fields.

Money. Probably the dead husband's money, too, and no tax paid on it. *Aha*, he thought. *A live one.*

A woman stumbled into the hall. She was about fifty, slim, with gray-blonde hair cut in a simple pageboy, wearing a rumpled madras shirtdress and boating moccasins. She said, "Who is it, Clarita?"

"A man from the State," Clarita said.

"Show him in," the woman said.

While she introduced herself as Myra Toddhunter,

Magaracz flashed his badge and gave her his card. From her breath Magaracz figured she'd had a couple of drinks, probably sherry or whatever it was these people drank. Pretty early in the morning but what the hell. "I'm here about your late husband's estate, Mrs. Toddhunter," he said.

She stifled a gasp, and leaned against the door frame, and said, "My husband — ! Has something happened to Edgar?" Magaracz got the idea that he had the wrong Toddhunter. "I'm sorry, Mrs. Toddhunter," he said. "It's the estate of Matthew Toddhunter we're investigating."

"Oh," she said. "Please come in and sit down."

"But if I've got the wrong —"

"Matthew Toddhunter was my son."

Gilmore appeared to Monica in the doorway of her kitchen, as she was clearing away the breakfast dishes. She looked up and there he stood.

There are times when the awareness of some fact or event explodes in the mind and blots out all other consciousness, the way a flashbulb exploding will blot out vision. *Gilmore is alive.*

She took a deep breath, molecules of the living Gilmore invading her nose and lungs, and let it out with a hiss, yoga breathing. Count four to inhale, six to exhale. Better with a cigarette.

"Don't smoke those things."

"Oh. Okay."

"Listen. I've come back to tell you something. I need you. I forgive you everything."

"You do?" *Don't smirk. If you smirk he'll hit you.*

"Monica, this is important."

This was important. A year and a half of raising the boys by herself, learning to do without him, thinking him dead, that wasn't important. But this was. Some concern of his was important. He glanced over his shoulder and came in, moving slowly, shutting the door behind him.

"Monica," he said, "I'm going to let you come back out west with me."

"Oh." Alive. Now, all at once and after all this time, she realized which one of them had actually . . .

"I want you and the boys to be all packed. Make sure the car's gas tank is full."

Had actually and in fact been mad all along. "Pack," she repeated. "Fill the gas tank." It was him, then, after all. She would tell that to Kevin. He would stop pestering her about undergoing therapy. She was certainly quite sane. Where was Kevin?

"The Jew will have to die, of course."

"Of course," she said. In the bathroom? At the store? She couldn't remember for some reason.

"It's a matter of honor," he said.

"I understand perfectly." Alive, and mad, and planning to murder Kevin. Well, but at least if he was alive . . .

"You've changed, Monica. You know that? You're truly worthy to be my wife now."

"Thank you, Gilmore." What lived could be killed. She could kill him. Since he was officially dead anyway, nobody would have to know.

He was strong, though, and fast. Best to get him suddenly from behind. Was there something heavy, or very sharp — ? She glanced over all the objects in the kitchen, evaluating everything. The paring knife was sharp, but too short to kill him instantly; she would have to hack at him. Not practical. The electric mixer was heavy enough, but he would notice her lifting it above his head. Mentally she rehearsed slaying him with everything her eyes passed over; she stuck him with forks; she brained him with frying pans; she ran hot water and soap into the sink and held his head under by the ears — no, the hair, she could get a better grip on it — until his breath stopped frothing up. But, no. All these things would take too long, and he would notice.

And then there would be the problem of disposing of the body. She wasn't ready to do that either. "Not now," she said.

"I'm sorry," Gilmore said. "This is all going too fast for you, isn't it? Well, listen. Take a day to get used to it. I'm coming back to you."

But, later, maybe. After she had a chance to collect her wits and form a plan. As long as the body was never found. Something that wouldn't be too nasty and revolting to carry out, something she could do alone, without involving Kevin. He was such an innocent.

"Pack your things," he said. "Be ready." He went to the door, opened it, and looked out.

"Yes, Gilmore." She would use her brains. Gilmore wasn't the only one who could get his way by using his intelligence. She would think of something.

"I will come for you in two days," he said, and silently he left.

Magaracz would have given a week's pay not to have to hear Myra Toddhunter's hard-luck story. He thought to spare himself that sort of thing, at least, when he gave up divorce work; the day he locked the door for the last time on his old office he said to himself, sure, he was giving up his independence, but at least he wouldn't have to deal with any more weeping women.

The son had killed himself.

He was a freshman at Princeton. His grades weren't as high as he expected, or he got involved with drugs, or queers, or politics, or Dungeons and Dragons, they never knew for sure what it was, and he swallowed a bottle of pills. Such a promising boy. Mrs. Toddhunter grew more and more hysterical as she told the sad story and ended by scrawling a check for the overdue estate tax and pushing it into Magaracz's hamlike hand. Now the check, so spotted with tears as to be scarcely legible, rested in his breast pocket. What a life. What a job.

Magaracz got out of there as fast as he could. Still no sign of the kid from the Bosnian Club; must have shaken him off somehow.

On an impulse, Magaracz got on the interstate and went to Pennsylvania, stopping only for doughnuts and coffee.

Conshohocken looked to Magaracz like a grubby little town, and the offices of Dr. Herman Eckes did nothing to dispel the impression. Magaracz went up the front steps and tried the door. It was locked. The bell didn't seem to make a noise inside, so he rapped sharply.

A woman in a shapeless flowered dress leaned out of the window above him. She wasn't wearing teeth.

"Doc ain't in," said the woman.

"When does he have office hours?" said Magaracz.

"Don't have no office hours. Last patient died last month. He, he."

"Shame," said Magaracz. "What'd he die of?"

"Heart failure."

"Um. Too bad. Will he be around anytime soon?"

"Tomorrow he comes for the rent."

"Oh. Okay. Tell him I was here, will you? Arthur Wottanobby. We're old buddies from the service."

"I'll tell him," she said.

The men who maintain the physical plant of the government of the State of New Jersey wear special coveralls, mostly of the same short-sleeved design, color-keyed to the sort of task they perform. Grounds keepers dress in green, for instance, and painters and plasterers in white, while the electricians all wear blue.

So it was that when Nick Magaracz boarded the elevator to go up to his office, he thought nothing of the bearded fellow getting on with him. He was there to work on the wiring. Magaracz would have known it even if he hadn't noticed the man's bag of tools.

The electrician had a cigar clamped in his teeth, one of those nasty little thin ones. It was lighted. From the tattoo on the man's arm Magaracz saw that he was a fellow ex-Marine. For the sake of the Corps he spoke to him softly and politely: "No smoking on these elevators, pal."

The man turned and looked at Magaracz with expressionless eyes. For an instant he nearly smiled.

Then he replied, in a voice even softer than the detective's, "Sorry about that, buddy. I guess I wasn't thinking." The car stopped on the third floor and he got out and walked down the hall. As the door rolled shut Magaracz could still hear the toolbag clinking.

NINE

THE TRAIN FROM Springfield came rolling and squeaking into the Trenton railroad station.

It was early morning, and Ruth Ann Walker, the bag lady who wore two pairs of glasses, was still asleep on a bench on the eastbound platform when six men got off the first passenger car. She felt the vibration of their tread, rather than heard them; they were walking in step, heavily and with authority. Ruth Ann opened one eye. She hadn't seen soldiers in Trenton since the fellows at Fort Dix had figured out that there wasn't anything to come here for.

They came up the platform toward her with the sun behind them, their shoulders bulking large. She sat up, shedding newspapers. Soldiers. Ruth Ann herself was dressed in a loose adaptation of Army fatigues, her latest style since she made a lucky find in the Rescue Mission's trash bin. She was pleased to see that no one had stolen her shoes. But it would be even nicer to start the morning with a cup of hot coffee and a cigarette.

"Hey!" she called to the men in her booming great voice. They had to pass right by her on their way to the moving stairs. "Hey! Soldiers!"

There was a stirring on the bench behind hers; an

old black man sat up and gave her a frown. "Hush," he said.

But Ruth Ann knew what soldiers were good for. "Hey! You got any cigarettes?"

The black man shook his head. "Let 'em alone," he whispered. "They ain't soldiers."

"Well, what then?" said Ruth Ann, indignant. The six men passed her bench, still tramping in step. "Say, you're Guardian Angels, aren't you?" she said to them. "How about a cigarette?"

"No," the first one growled. He had hard eyes, set close together, the better to look down the neck of a Coke bottle. Things poked out of the sides of the canvas duffels they all carried. Guns, maybe, or badminton rackets.

The rest of the men pretended to ignore her, except for one, who remarked, "Her kind will be the first to go, when the new order comes."

They went up the moving stairs, still marching. She shouted after them: "Says you, buster!" Then she picked up her newspapers and arranged them on herself again. Time for a little more shut-eye. "The new order, huh? What are they gonna do to me that the old order didn't?" she said.

"Right on, sister," said the old man. "You and me both." She lay down and dozed off again.

Nick Magaracz's office did not face the railroad station, though if it had he could almost have seen it, if not for the new high-rise office buildings springing up like box-shaped mushrooms on the intervening parking lots. Instead he overlooked the old Hessian Barracks.

Trenton, like any eastern town of its size, has many

aspects. It is, among other things, the site of one of the most important battles of the Revolutionary War. One Christmas Eve a company of drunken Hessian mercenaries was overwhelmed in that very barracks by Washington's forces, which had just crossed the Delaware.

Magaracz had no particular interest in the historical significance of the Hessian Barracks, since as far as he knew his own forebears had been trying to grow potatoes in eastern Europe at the time, but he was grateful for the fact that the barracks had been preserved along with their cool green lawn and trees. The view from the window beside the office coffee maker was one of the finest in Trenton. The alternative to the barracks would have been another office building competing for sun, air, and parking spaces.

Magaracz left the window with a sigh and took his coffee back to his little steel-and-burlap cube. He found it just possible to get comfortable there by pulling out the bottom drawer of his desk (a shelf with drawers, fixed to the wall of the cube by precarious hooks) and resting his feet in it, although this practice tended to mash the file folders. He did it now. On his so-called desk was his official to-do list. He took it up and prepared to revise his priorities the way the State had taught him in time management class.

Cross out the visit to Matthew Toddhunter's heirs. The fluorescent ceiling light over his desk was flickering again. He wrote on the to-do list:

Try again to requisition a desk lamp.

A shadow fell between Magaracz and the faltering fluorescent fixture. He looked up to see a stocky middle-aged man in a raincoat standing over him.

"Mr. Magaracz?" the man said.

"Yes," Magaracz acknowledged. The man looked like FBI, somehow, probably the raincoat, and his ID confirmed it. "Special Agent Lucas," he said. "I understand you've been making inquiries about a certain individual by the name of Gilmore Nash."

"Right," said Magaracz.

"We at the Bureau would like you to lay off for a little while. Find something else to do."

"What for?" said Magaracz.

Lucas paused for a moment, either thinking how to get a handle on Magaracz or deciding how much it was okay to tell him. "What's the purpose of your investigation, Mr. Magaracz?" he said at last.

"Possibility of inheritance tax fraud."

"You're wasting your time," Lucas said. "I can't put it any more plainly than that. The State of New Jersey will never be a dime richer on Gilmore Nash's inheritance tax. Trust me. Find another case to go after."

"What's the story?"

"I'm sorry," said Lucas, "I can't tell you any more than I already have. But as a professional courtesy, I'm asking you to let it go for a while. Thank you very much for your cooperation." He left as silently as he had come.

So the feds wanted him to lay off. The last time they gave him advice like that was when he was still a P.I., going up against a protected Mafia witness who was harassing a sweet young client. Then, he had ignored the advice. Maybe he would this time too. But he would be discreet.

At the top of his to-do list it said, *Run a police check on Nash.* He hadn't done it yet. Wonder how the FBI knew he was on Nash's case. Discreetly, he

85

picked up the phone and dialed Trenton Police Head-quarters. Even more discreetly he asked to speak to Frank Fennuccio, his wife's younger brother, recently promoted to detective.

"Yo," said Fennuch.

"It's Nick," said Magaracz. "I need a favor, my man."

"Shoot."

"There's a guy who's supposed to have died a year and a half ago, name of Gilmore Nash." Magaracz read off his address and Social Security number. "Can you run a check on him, without letting anyone know it's for me?"

"Sure."

"Thanks."

"I'll get back to you."

Art Pacewick appeared in the cubicle entrance.

"How are you doing with the estate tax investigation?" he said.

"Fine," said Magaracz, and smiled at him in silence for a while.

"You're not going to fool with the Nash case anymore," Pacewick said.

"I'm not?"

"No, Nick. Probably it's a waste of your time anyway. But the FBI . . ."

"They got to you, huh?" said Magaracz.

"The State Treasurer gave me a call this afternoon and told me to pull you off the case."

"Nobody wants me on the case. I wonder how come."

"Nick," said Pacewick, sitting down, "I'm going to tell you a little story. Once upon a time I used to work for Intertec."

"As an operative?" said Magaracz, surprised.

"Why, yes. As an operative. I was making pretty

good money, and the work was kind of fun, and I liked my job a lot. I got to travel, chase bad guys, the whole thing."

"And then?"

"Well, one day I found out that the guy who was supervising me was taking graft. I didn't like that. It didn't seem right."

"So what did you do?"

"Blew the whistle on him. Only somehow it got to be my fault, and they canned my ass out on the street, with four daughters to support. Ten years I worked for Intertec. No severance pay, nothing. I was out of a job eighteen months after that. My wife had to go back to work, with the baby still in diapers."

"So what you're saying is . . ."

"Cover your ass, Nick. I tell you this as a friend. These guys want you to lay off, lay off. The Treasurer told me to tell you lay off. I'm telling you. Lay off."

TEN

WHEN THE MAIL came around, Magaracz found his résumé and his check returned from *Modern Warrior* magazine, along with a little note saying that this box number was no longer active. *They're rolling it up*, he thought. But what was it? And who were they?

He dialed the number of the classified advertising department of *Modern Warrior*. It was in Phoenix, Arizona, and Pacewick would give him a hard time about it when the bill came in, but that wouldn't be for another month. Maybe by then Magaracz would have landed his job in industrial espionage. The field was getting hot. Somebody told him there was an article about it in the *New York Times* just the other day.

"*Modern Warrior*."

"Hello, miss, I'd like to renew an ad that I ran the month before last in the classified."

"Your name and address, sir?"

"My address is changed. That's part of the reason I'm calling. But I don't want any change in the ad; it's fine just the way it is. You'll have it listed under Box 13230."

A rattle of terminal keys as the woman addressed

her computer. "Very well, Dr. Eckes," she said. "But the ad won't go back in until two months from now. Will that be all right? And I'm afraid our rates have gone up."

"That's fine," said Magaracz.

"And you no longer want the bill and any responses sent to Conshohocken?"

"No, send them care of the Bosnian-American Social Club, R.F.D. 1, Titusville, New Jersey."

The keys clacked softly. "Is there a zip on that?" He didn't know the zip code for Titusville. He made one up. She thanked him and he hung up the phone.

Eckes. What was his game?

Marcia came in with the latest printout. "Lucky I put all those records on a disk file," she said. "It's a mess down there. They say it'll be another week before they're able to handle any more tapes, what with having to sort out the master files by hand. Rory Valentine has left, and they're going to have to train another I/O specialist on this system."

"Too bad," said Nick.

"No, it was just as well," she said. "He was coming in drunk in the afternoon and messing the jobs up."

"So how did your test turn out?" Magaracz said.

"You'll be interested to know," she said, handing the printout to him, "that most of the dead are men between the ages of eighteen and forty-five."

"An army of dead guys," Magaracz said. What was the racket? Zombies? A zombie army?

"And the funerals were almost all handled by the same people. But I'll let you see it for yourself. It's very interesting."

"Batt's Funeral Home," said Magaracz. "And most

of them died of heart failure, or accidents of some kind. Where Dr. Eckes just happened to be on the scene."

"Here's a drug overdose. Matthew Toddhunter. Eighteen years old."

"No kidding," said Magaracz.

"The zip codes don't seem to be statistically significant," she said.

"That's okay," said Magaracz. "They'll be plenty significant when I have to start chasing all over the state following this stuff up."

Magaracz met his brother-in-law at the Neon Bar and Grill. They had good hamburgers and the draft beer was reasonably priced.

He found Fennuccio waiting for him at a table in front by the window. "So what's the story on this guy Nash?" he asked Fennuccio. "Is he a wanted felon, or what?"

"Your friend is quite a boy," Fennuccio said. "Ever hear of the Posse Comitatus?"

"A radical right-wing tax revolt organization," Magaracz said. "Nash was a member. They illegal?"

"Bombing an assemblyman's house is illegal, even in Oregon," Fennuccio said. "How about the Committee for Patriotic Christian Action?"

"You got me there," said Magaracz.

"Radical right-wing antiabortionists. Blew up seven clinics, killed three doctors and a number of nurses, injured a lot more people. One lady is still in a coma in a burn trauma unit in Eugene."

"Gilmore Nash had something to do with all this?" said Magaracz.

"Strong suspect. Also a Hebrew school in Portland, not to mention a police station, where law enforcement officers like you and me got blown to hamburger."

"Like you, Fennuch. I myself am a state worker." Magaracz downed his beer.

"Whatever. The feds were hot after him, and they almost had enough on him to put him away, when he cashed, not far from here, as I guess you know. What's up?"

"I think maybe he's still around. Maybe still around Trenton."

"Terrific," said Fennuccio. "That's just what Trenton needs right now is a mad bomber."

The two stared out into the gray and rainy street, ruminating in silence on the prospect of a rash of bombings.

"Well, Nick, what do you think he'll go for?" Fennuccio said.

"Offhand I can think of three synagogues, maybe Planned Parenthood, Mercer Hospital . . . . You say he hit a police station?"

"The FBI says it."

"Okay, the police station — that's your office — the Taxation building — that's my office —"

Traffic was passing by, splashing muddy water onto the sidewalk across the street. Hardly anyone was out. In the entrance to an alley a familiar beak poked out of an olive-drab poncho hood. The Ace was standing soaked up to his knees, watching the door of the Neon.

"Look at that kid," said Magaracz, gesturing with the remains of his sandwich. "He's been tailing me all weekend. Last night he slept in my yard."

"Let's go get him," Fennuccio said. "Bring him in here and buy him a beer. Maybe he'll tell us what he wants."

"Okay," said Magaracz. "Sounds good to me. I'll slip out the side door and sneak up on him, and you go out the front."

But even as they were making their plan they saw three local kids go up and surround The Nose where he stood against the wall. There were menacing motions, a glint that could have been a knife, a blow. Before Magaracz and his brother-in-law could get up from their seats it was over.

"See that?" Fennuccio said, springing to his feet. "Let's get 'em." But the three locals were off toward Perry Street at the speed of light. The kid sat on a crate holding his head, his pockets ripped, his watch gone.

"Come on," Fennuccio said, fishing in his pocket for some bills. As he threw them on the table a truck stopped in traffic and obscured their view of the alley. When it moved on a moment later the kid was gone.

"Psst. Marge," said the young fellow working the cash register at the Ewing Shop-Rite.

"What is it, Eddie?"

"It's her. It's Drano Woman. She's here again."

"What woman?" said Marge. "That's a guy. With a moustache." But there was something feminine about the bearing of the fellow who had just come in, his walk, maybe, or the shape of his rear end as the two clerks followed him with their eyes up the household products aisle.

"I tell you it's her," said Eddie, "wearing another wig and a moustache this time. You watch. She'll come back to the checkout counter with nothing but three cans of Drano."

And she did.

Batt's Funeral Home was in Ewing Township, Magaracz remembered. It was one of those new places, looking sort of like a dignified dry cleaner's; the old Batt's was a Victorian mansion in the middle of Trenton, torn down for a high-rise old folks' home while Joseph Batt, senior, was still alive. Junior was running it these days. Magaracz remembered him from senior year at Trenton Catholic Boys' High; he used to like to do things to squirrels.

Magaracz went in and asked to see him.

Nobody was there except young Joseph Batt's widowed mother, as sweet an old lady as Magaracz had ever seen. Surely she couldn't be involved in anything crooked. He asked her if Joe was around.

"My son is visiting friends in Illinois," she said. "We're referring people to another establishment until he comes back next week. Unless you're a relative of Mr. Badger."

"Uh, yeah," Magaracz said. "Uh, as a matter of fact, I — uh — was wondering if it would be okay if I —"

She patted his hand. "You may come and see the departed," she said. "It's quite all right." She took him down to the lower depths, where the cold room was.

"I don't know whether you're aware of it," she said, turning on the light, "but Mr. Badger left written instructions that in the event of his demise no one was to handle his final arrangements but my son. That's why he's still here; he's waiting for Joe to come back."

Small feet, thought Magaracz. She sighed and drew

back the sheet that covered Badger's face; he still looked blue. "I hope you have no objection," she said. "Of course the wishes of the survivors must be considered in these cases, but as no one came forward, we thought —"

"No, no," said Magaracz. "That's fine. I just — It was so hard for me to believe, when I heard that Os was gone —"

"I quite understand," said the old lady. She covered the stiff, and turned the light out, and they started up the stairs again.

"What were the details of the arrangements that Cousin Os wanted?" Magaracz said. "Just so I can tell the relatives on the West Coast, you understand."

She said, "Your cousin left written, signed instructions that he was to be cremated and his ashes thrown to the four winds."

"The four winds again," Magaracz said. "Always the four winds, never the seven seas. Why do you suppose that is?"

She looked at him curiously. "Perhaps they don't like to be wet," she said.

"These guys that drowned in the bear-hunting accident in Maine," said Magaracz. "Did they go with the four winds?"

"What do you mean?"

"Murchison, Ritter, Harkness, and Stout. Did your son handle their final arrangements, by any chance?"

"I'm afraid I have no idea. Is there something wrong?"

"I hope not," said Magaracz. "I'd like to talk to your son, though, when he gets back." He gave her his card. The look she gave him would have taken your skin off.

"Bureau of Tax Enforcement," she read.

"Just ask him to call me, please," said Magaracz.

There was a new diner out by the airport called the Four Winds. It would have been too good to find all the dead men ranged around the horseshoe-shaped counter, eating and drinking and discussing their next adventure; it would have been too good, and it was. But the pie they had there was the best that Magaracz had eaten since the last one Ethel made, and the coffee was passable, and he went on his way refreshed.

ELEVEN

DR. ECKES HAD spent a disquieting day in Conshohocken. The real estate agent had failed to make a quick sale of his properties, two tenants had flitted owing several months' rent, and old Mrs. Mulrooney had babbled something at him about an Army buddy looking him up. Eckes was never in the Army. It made him uneasy, and he had an extra hour to think about it when a gravel truck turned over and stopped all the traffic on Interstate 95.

The last thing he needed to hear when he finally got back to the Bosnian Club was the news that the Hedervary sisters were imprisoned in the cellar.

"I was mugged in Trenton today," said the Ace, "and so here was Gil Nash in the kitchen helping me put ice on my head. One of the sisters came in and saw him. They recognized him right away, and they started yelling and everything. Gil picked up the butcher knife. I thought he was going to carve them up right there on the kitchen floor till Bill Sherbrook made him put it away."

"Wonder what it was to Sherbrook?" said the doctor, with a frown of annoyance.

"He likes them. You know, they're not so bad. So

96

Sherbrook said it would be enough to get them out of the way for a couple of days. He took them down and locked them in the cellar."

"What are they doing?"

"Just being very quiet. Sherbrook told them he'd bring them some food later, and then he went to the supermarket, I think. They won't eat any of our food. He had to get them special stuff."

"Tcha!" said the doctor.

"Also a couple of men called from the New Zinderneuf Trap Rock Company. They said the zoning variance was all fixed and for you to set a date with them for the closing."

"It's all falling in place very nicely," the doctor said. "Except for those two old hens. Shame about that. We can't even bury them down there; New Zinderneuf would dig them up too soon." He sighed. Sometimes the burdens of leadership were enormous.

In the parish house of Saint Joachim's, Ethel Magaracz was looking for the Hedervary sisters. Never before had they missed a regular meeting of the Altar Rosary Society.

Maybe something's happened to them, she thought. She called the sisters' house. No answer. Dreadful images ran through Ethel's mind of the poor old souls collapsed at the foot of the stairs with their legs broken, or worse. The house was a block and a half away. Ethel hiked over and knocked on the door.

No sounds of distant moaning answered her knock. Not home? Unconscious? She went back to the parish house and telephoned Nick. He could break in and look for them, and if they weren't there he would know what to do next.

They weren't there. Magaracz figured they were still at the Bosnian Club, where he was forbidden to go. But that was on State time. He guessed he could go there on his own time. The worst that could happen was that he could get hurt, and the State would refuse to pay him sick leave injury benefits because he wasn't on the job.

Or the worst that could happen was that Special Agent Lucas could shoot him. Then Art Pacewick would come to the viewing and say, "I told you so."

He parked the Thunderbird on a turnoff down the road from the club, out of sight, as close as he could get and still sneak up on them. He got out and began to make his way over the top of the hill and through the trees.

There was still some daylight left, enough, Magaracz figured, for him to see his way through the woods to the club. It was one of those nasty little woods where the trees were too thin to hide behind. As he gained the crest of the hill, wheezing and puffing, he began to have an uneasy feeling about the lack of cover. He got down and crept, very carefully.

After a long time he found himself crouching behind a small cinder-block building at the edge of a clearing, none other than the men's comfort station of the Bosnian-American Social Club picnic ground. The clubhouse was maybe fifty yards away. One light was on in the clubhouse; a little smoke drifted out of the chimney and trailed in low wisps over the field. A sign of more bad weather.

Moving slowly and quietly, keeping down, Magaracz approached the Bosnian clubhouse until he came right up to what seemed to be the kitchen door. Pausing, he thought suddenly that he heard someone breathing not far away from him, soft menacing breaths. Like a shot he dropped down into the shadow of the back steps, hiding almost under them.

Magaracz found his elbow resting against what felt like a man's shoulder encased in a nylon jacket. He started violently, banging his head on the steps.

"Dwayne?" called a voice in the kitchen. "That you?"

When there was no answer, the man in the kitchen grunted and walked away. Magaracz could hear his clumping footsteps receding. He put his hand out then to feel what he expected to be a dead body, and discovered instead a gym bag. The shoes had felt like shoulder bones.

They were combat boots, small, maybe size eight. Where had he seen something about size eight combat boots? Also there were three turtleneck shirts, and some other clothes. Magaracz had a sudden hunch. He held the leg of one of the pairs of trousers out where the light could reach it. Sure enough. Camouflage cloth.

Then someone stepped up and stuck what felt like a gun barrel into the back of his left ear.

The official vehicle of the Bosnian-American Social Club was a dark green Dodge van with a white magnetic sign on the side that said "Bosnian-American Club" in red and black letters and a bumper sticker on the back with a black silhouette of a Saturday-night-special handgun and the words "My Right." Dwayne had put the sticker there because he didn't have a car of his own. The others had left it, even though it was not a precise statement of the political philosophy of the group. The Ace, for instance, would have needed a much longer sticker to express his political thought, and the doctor found it lacking because it didn't mention taxes. As far as Dwayne himself was concerned the message of the bumper sticker might even have been excessively complex.

But Dwayne wasn't here. Gilmore Nash had invited only the Ace and Dr. Eckes to perform the delicate task of putting the final radio-controlled explosive charges into the Taxation building.

Eckes drove. There was some desultory conversation about their plans for the future. The Ace seemed to be angling for an invitation to join the doctor at his ranch in Argentina. "When will you go down there?" the Ace asked.

"As soon as the deal with New Zinderneuf Trap Rock is complete. I'll let my Conshohocken properties go." He figured to get out of paying state sales tax on the clubhouse and grounds. "No one will have to, after this," he said, and Nash could see his smile in the lights of passing cars, the smile of an admiral sailing into a conquered harbor. He was driving with one hand.

"Don't get overconfident," Nash advised. "That's how mistakes get made."

"Are you still sulking because I wouldn't let you bring the dogs to town?" the doctor said.

"I think it was a mistake to leave the dogs," said Nash. "Dogs can be useful."

"I detest driving with dogs," the doctor said. "They stink and they drool down the back of my neck. And then every time we pass a black person on the street they hang out the window and go a-woof-a-woof-a-

100

woof-a at the tops of their voices until everyone within three blocks is staring."

Gilmore Nash tuned his colleague out, and let his mind wander into pleasant fantasies of how it would be when the Taxation building went up.

He had planned this carefully, and meant for it to be his finest job. The things he had done in Nam were of necessity slapdash, and the works he performed in Oregon, while there was plenty of time to do them right, had not been adequately funded. This was the first time he had ever worked with both time enough and money.

Since the first string of firecrackers that ever he found under a Christmas tree, Gilmore Nash had been fascinated with the art of creating explosions. There were all kinds: sappers, which done right would look sound enough afterward to lure the unwary onto the weak part of the target object (usually a bridge), whereupon it would collapse all at once; whammers, where the target was blasted into flaming debris to fly in all directions; and folders, his favorite.

A properly done folder was achieved not with one charge but with many, planted at strategic points all over the target structure. By setting these charges off at carefully timed intervals, the demolition expert could cause the structure to fold in on itself like a flower closing at evening.

With the detonator now in his hands, a unit of his own design set to send radio signals on twenty different frequencies, Gilmore Nash meant to create such a precisely tuned demolition as to beggar everything that had gone before. Not even an ash, he expected, would fall on the sidewalk outside; but whatever was inside would be reduced to powder in ninety-three seconds.

Eckes parked the van in front of the State House, just out of sight of their target. The three of them donned the state worker coveralls that Nash provided. Then they took their drills and their handfuls of prepared explosive charges, the size and shape of cigars, and went to plug them into the Tax building. Only a few cylinders needed to be inserted into the building's supporting structure. If the others thought it strange that there was so little to do to finish the job, they never said anything about it to Nash. He had, of course, performed the inside work already, some of it even before the rest of them had made the decision to go ahead with the demolition. *But that's what happens,* he reflected. *People who know what they want get their way.*

It went quickly. Nash was finished first. As he slipped his last cylinder into its warm little hole, he heard the crash of breaking glass.

The van was being robbed.

TWELVE

MAGARACZ HAD been thrown in the cellar with the old ladies. It was completely dark. They had put handcuffs on his wrists and ankles and rolled him rudely down the steps. He told the Hedervary sisters who he was, and they were relieved to have him there, though he wasn't going to be much use chained up.

"If only we could make a hole in this door somehow," Maria fretted, "perhaps I could shoot through it. I know I could hit one of those men in some vital spot."

"Shoot what?" said Magaracz, his scalp beginning to crawl.

Ruza clucked her tongue. "Apparently those men keep their guns and ammunition down here," she sighed. "We found some things in boxes. Would you like a bulletproof vest?"

"Not with these handcuffs on," he said. "Couldn't get my arms in it. You say you have guns?"

"They're all in pieces," Ruza said. "Maria is putting them together. I don't like guns."

"Guns are a good thing in their place," Maria said. Small clicks and clinks were coming from her corner. "But as you know, Mr. Magaracz, you have to handle

103

them with respect. Firearms can be quite dangerous if not correctly handled."

"I believe it," he said. "I don't like to carry them, myself. What kind of gun are we talking about, anyway?"

"I think this must be an Ingram MAC Ten," said Maria. "It's not something I'm familiar with, but I think perhaps I can manage. . . . You know, I don't believe this weapon has a sight."

"Sight?" Magaracz said. "Are you kidding? Does a can of Raid have a sight? You point it in the general direction of your exterminee and spray. A thousand rounds a minute, they tell me."

"Lacks finesse," said Maria.

"That it does. Are you sure you know how to work that thing? Aagh." Something with a lot of legs walked across his nose. He shook his head and banged it by mistake on a rock in the dirt floor. Stars pricked the blackness.

"I wonder," he said, "if one of you ladies would help me sit up. I think my back is out. I've got a thousand-legger on my face."

Ruza Hedervary gave a shriek.

"Help the man, Ruza," Maria said. "I've almost got this together, and I don't want to take my fingers off it." There were more clicking noises.

"I'm sorry," Ruza said. "It's just that I'm afraid of thousand-leggers. Where are you?"

"Here," Magaracz said. Hands felt him and pulled him to sit upright. He leaned against a wooden box.

"I don't suppose you ladies would know where there's anything like a file down here."

"What for?" said Ruza.

"Handcuffs," he said.

"Not a file, no," said Maria, "but if you want something to cut handcuffs, why not try the corner of the stone foundation, where the door is?"

Magaracz scooted over toward the door, propelled by heels, bottom, and knuckles. There was a stone corner. He turned his back to it. The edge felt rough enough.

He began to saw.

Maybe in a few hours the stone would bite through the handcuffs. Would that be time enough? For what? What was going on? As he worked, Magaracz considered whether he shouldn't be doing the cuffs on his feet instead, so he could run better. Clicks and grunts from Maria.

"Ruza, be a dear and feel around in those boxes for some magazines, will you? I think I almost have this together."

"Magazines?"

"Clips of bullets. Rectangular pieces of metal. You'll be able to feel the little bullet nose at the top of one side. Get me a few, when you find them."

"Oh. All right, dear."

Bumps and creaks.

"And be careful not to jostle anything," Maria added. "When Mr. Sherbrook had the door open putting us down here I saw that a lot of those boxes said 'explosives.' "

"Where is he, by the way?" said Ruza. "Do you think he was fibbing to us about dinner? I really feel very hungry. Was it he who caught you, do you think, Mr. Magaracz? Or one of the others?"

"It was a couple of guys I never saw before," Magaracz said. "They were all dressed up in sheriffs' outfits."

"One of them will come back sooner or later," said Maria. "And when he does, I'll shoot him. There. It's all together now."

"Shoot the lock, why don't you?" Magaracz said. "After I get away from this door, that is."

Maria said, "No. It might ricochet and strike the dynamite, or one of us."

"Well, don't shoot anybody unless you have to. Just tell him you got him covered and he better watch his ass."

"Oh, very well," she said. "But you know, it might come to shooting just the same. When they come I want you to be sure to get well away from the doorway. I've never fired one of these."

Magaracz suddenly thought of the time he had rented a belt sander to do his living room floor, how it had bucked and jolted. "Tell you what," he said. "Hold off on firing that thing and I'll take you to a real neat shooting range I know when we get out of here. All the cops go there."

"Tsk," she said. He wasn't sure whether she was agreeing or not.

106

THIRTEEN

THE THREE MEN ran the half-block to the Bosnian Club van. The dome light was on, illuminating a large teenager hacking at the dashboard with a screwdriver. They shouted at him: "Hey! Get out of there!" and he jumped out the driver's side into the street. There was no traffic. He went up a stairway between two buildings, running with surprising speed.

Nash glanced in the broken window of the van and saw that the front seat was completely empty. "Son of a bitch got the detonator," he called to the others. "Let's get after him." He pelted across the street and up the steps.

The others followed him. The steps led to a parking lot that gave out onto Capitol Alley. No sign of the thief; he could have gone any of three ways.

"Split up and look for him," said Nash. "If I'm not at the truck in half an hour you go back to the club without me."

"Right," said the others.

So they separated, and all lost track of the others.

Monica stamped the mud off her boots and shook the rain out of her curling hair. The house was warm,

107

and welcomed her with food smells as she fumbled in her clothes for a cigarette. The boys had cooked hamburgers. They began to complain at her.

"Where were you, Mom?" said Henry.

"Where were you?" Scott said. "It's dark out. We didn't know where you were."

"I thought I'd go for a little walk in the woods," said Monica. "It's nice out."

"No, it isn't," said Scott. "It's raining again."

"Well, I thought it was nice," said Monica. It had been nice, up on the hill under the trees, dumping her Drano into the old freezer. That freezer had been a landmark in the woods for such a long time, all shot up with shotgun blasts (but never pierced; it was still watertight) that nobody really saw it anymore. It was perfect. She was very excited about her plan. Her breath was coming a little fast. At last she was taking her fate into her own hands.

Now to dissolve the pills.

Fatman of Fatman's Bar looked up to see one of his occasional patrons, a young junkie they called Tyrone, coming in the door carrying a thing under his arm that might have been a piece of audio equipment or a fancy cable tuner. He put the thing on the bar and began to drum with his fingers, rolling his eyes over his shoulder and sniffling.

"What you got there, son?"

"Steereo," said Tyrone.

"Don't look like much," Fatman observed.

"She-it," said Tyrone. "Mofo steereo. Worf a hunnerd. Snufff."

Fatman took the appliance in his hands, turned it over a couple of times and pressed one of the twenty buttons. There was a loud bang in the distance. Children had no kind of discipline these days; when Fatman was a boy, he always saved up his firecrackers for the Fourth of July. "I'll give you ten for it," he said to Tyrone, and produced a ten-dollar bill.

"She-it." Tyrone took the ten and ran out, leaving the appliance on the bar. The transaction was complete. Fatman tucked it down among the rest and forgot about it.

FOURTEEN

WHEN THE SUN comes up on a June morning in the little hills north of Trenton, the first sound to be heard is of birds, tweeting and caroling, and then maybe a small flock of crows calling loud caws as they wheel through the air on their early morning rounds. The cool, damp mist of night begins to lift and burn away in the light of a sun that will be scorching later on.

The bats, the rats and mice, the possums, all find their homes and sleep; but the creatures of the day rise and stretch and go outside to empty their bladders on the dewy grass. And so it was with Gilmore Nash's Dobermans.

Nash went with them this morning. He had returned on foot in the small hours, finding only Dwayne and the Ace still awake. They half-expected him to be carrying the dismembered body of the thief in his jaws, but he had to tell them he never found the guy.

"What were you doing all that time?" said the Ace.

"Making arrangements," said Nash. And so he had been. To be exact, he had been breaking into a hobby store and stealing a radio-control unit for model airplanes, with which, if he could get close enough, he could set off the explosives in the Tax building. It would be far cruder than what he had planned, but it would do.

"I had to hot-wire the van," the Ace complained. "Doc had the keys."

"He wasn't with you?" Nash said.

"I thought he was with you."

"You know," Nash said, "I'd get rid of those if I were you."

The Ace realized he still had two radio-controlled charges in his shirt pocket. "Oh, okay," he said. "I'll take care of it right after breakfast."

"Suit yourself," Nash said. "But if some guy with a dirty-signal CB comes by here he could set those charges off. One'd be all it would take to kill you."

"I wonder if the doc knows that," the Ace said. "He had three in his pocket the last time I saw him." He went outside and threw them as far as he could in the woods.

"Want some coffee?" Dwayne asked. "It'll be done in a minute."

"No, thanks," said Nash. "I'll get some where I'm going." It was time now to go back to his wife and complete his plan. "See you around," he said, and he took his dogs and his bicycle and set out for the old house.

Magaracz and the Hedervarys could hear the men, getting breakfast, as it seemed, over their heads; something was sizzling appealingly, and there was music on the radio.

"Maybe they'll give us breakfast," Ruza said hopefully.

The music stopped, and an announcer began to read the morning news. "The body of an unidentified man

111

was found late last night in the two hundred block of West Hanover Street in Trenton," said the news announcer, "evidently the victim of an accident involving fireworks, which are illegal in our city. Police are seeking information as to the identity of the man, who was white, in late middle age, five feet eleven inches tall, wearing a pair of dark blue coveralls, black socks, and brown wing-tip shoes."

"Oh, my God!" one of the men upstairs roared. "The doctor is dead!"

There were sounds of distress from above them, low moaning and murmurs. One of the men was sobbing. Somebody stamped on the floor.

"Dead," said Ruza. "Imagine that."

"Good riddance to bad rubbish," said Maria.

"But what are these yahoos going to do without a leader?" Magaracz wondered.

"With us, you mean."

"Yeah, now that you mention it. With us."

The cellar door creaked open then, and the light of morning surrounded the slight figure of Bill Sherbrook, the guard. The sisters drew closer together, and Magaracz tried to get behind their bulletproof vests.

"I'm going to shoot you now," Maria Hedervary said.

"Hey, don't do that," called Sherbrook. "I came to get you out. Special Agent Sherbrook, FBI." His voice reverberated in the cavernous cellar.

"Mr. Sherbrook," said Ruza. "Where have you been? I want my dinner."

The sound of footsteps and voices overhead had stopped. They began to whisper.

"I hope you don't mind," Magaracz hissed, "but I'd kind of like to see some credentials."

"Magaracz, you asshole, are you here?" the FBI man said, coming down the cellar steps. "I thought Lucas told you to stay away from this place."

"Who are you calling an asshole?" said Magaracz.

Maria said, "Oh, please."

"Sorry, ladies," Sherbrook murmured. "Magaracz, what's the matter with you, anyhow?"

"I'm handcuffed," said Magaracz. "Do you have a key to these things?"

"Yeah, I think this key'll fit," said the FBI man. He fiddled with the handcuffs without being able to see them. The cuffs on Magaracz's ankles yielded at once, but the other pair seemed to take longer. "The key doesn't fit these," said Sherbrook. "Let's just get out of here as fast as we can." He went up the steps. "Come on, all of you."

Maria followed him, and then Ruza, and last of all Magaracz, who figured there was less chance that way of getting his rear end shot off by Maria.

As Sherbrook emerged from the Bosnian Club cellar the men from the clubhouse closed in.

"So! FBI!" said one. "You dirty traitor!"

Blam! A gun went off. Sherbrook fell down the steps on top of Ruza. "Shit," he said, and died.

Maria let go with the MAC Ten.

There was a terrific racket, the submachine gun chattering, guys screaming.

It was some kind of gun, Magaracz had to admit. Never had he seen so many bullets flying at once, or heard so much noise, not even in Korea. One of the men must have been killed outright, and the others ducked out of sight someplace; impossible to tell whether they'd been hit. Somebody behind the back porch fired off a few rounds. Maria returned the fire.

113

Splinters flew. Maria was still standing up there. Magaracz could see only the lower part of her body; the upper part was hanging out of the cellar door, encased in bulletproofing, as she trained the MAC Ten on the yard. He became very keenly aware of the pattern on her dress, small white birds on a gray background, and of the veins in the back of her legs, and her stockings, rolled above the knee in round garters, and the stout black shoes.

We're all gonna die, he thought, *and me in handcuffs.*

But the gunfire had stopped. Instead, there was a sound overhead of ripping wood, and nails being torn screaming from the joists. Looking up, Magaracz saw the tip of a crowbar sticking between the floorboards and prying. *Christ, they're coming through the ceiling.*

"Let's get out of here," he suggested to the ladies. Ruza, unhurt, got out from under Sherbrook's body and stood up.

"Follow me, I'll cover you," Maria said, and they did, hunched over and running low across the lawn. At the edge of the woods she motioned them into the bushes, then turned and fired her weapon again, putting out every window on that side of the clubhouse.

"Tsk," said Ruza. "We'll only have to repair those, you know."

"No, we won't," her sister said. "Now that the doctor's gone we'll sell it."

"But . . ."

"Let's go. They're coming after us."

Monica had made a hot, nourishing breakfast of waffles and scrambled eggs. The boys were all dressed, their lunches packed. When the school bus came they would be all ready. They were sitting in the untidy

114

living room catching a little morning TV, when she thought she heard a sound out back.

Without disturbing the boys, who were raptly gazing at a noisy cartoon show, she made her way through the kitchen and opened the back door.

Sure enough, there stood Gilmore.

"Have you prepared the boys?" he asked.

Prepared them? Ah, yes. They have been tenderly broiled, and Sauce Béchamel dribbled over their bodies. "Drink this," she said bluntly, handing him the cup of doped coffee. To her astonishment he drank it, and fell to the floor like a sack of rocks.

"What was that?" called Henry.

"I dropped the garbage," said Monica. "Do you want to help me carry it out?"

"In a minute," the boy replied. She knew he wouldn't come.

Gilmore began to snore. She took his legs, one under each arm, and dragged him out the back door and down the steps. His sneakers were completely worn out. How stupid, when he had a whole box of perfectly good shoes in the attic.

Bang! went his head on the flagstone. *Did he feel that?* No matter. But surely there was a better way to carry him. Ten feet farther on she began to feel tired.

She sat down on the stump of the old oak tree that the gypsy caterpillars had eaten to death the year before and stared at him.

A bubble of excitement rose in her chest. She lit a cigarette unsteadily. Success within her grasp. Nothing left to do but drag him up the hill and cast him into the freezer. Maybe with a rug or an old sheet wrapped around him he would be easier to pull.

But first she would sit on the stump and smoke for

a while, enjoying the morning, thinking how his flesh would hiss when she dropped him in. No more Gilmore. Free at last.

The dogs, Pickles and Baldy, came running out of the woods, sniffed the body of their master, whimpered, and then sat down at Monica's feet, crossing their front paws and sighing.

FIFTEEN

MAGARACZ AND THE Hedervarys were running along a path through the woods. From time to time the bad guys took a shot at them, but Maria had them badly outgunned with the Ingram. They had only a couple of ordinary handguns, something that fired one shot at a time and needed frequent reloading. Maria had only to spray the bushes, a thousand rounds a minute if the gun didn't jam. Once there was a scream and a crash of branches. "Got another one," she said.

"How much ammo does that baby hold, anyhow?" asked Magaracz.

"I brought some extra clips," she said. "I also took the precaution of disabling the ones we left behind."

"Good girl," he said.

"I know we'll come to a house soon," said Ruza. "The road is this way. We can telephone the police from there." Magaracz expected any minute to hear police helicopters, or at least game wardens coming after them, they were making so much racket.

"I guess we're way out in the woods," he said. "Otherwise it seems like they'd already be here." They ducked down behind a big rock for a moment to rest. Maria peered cautiously over the top.

"No place in New Jersey is that far out in the woods," she said. "Certainly not in this part of the state. That's why it's against the law to hunt with a rifle here."

"I'm not a hunting man, myself," Magaracz said. "My father-in-law hunts."

"Let's go," said Maria. Magaracz never knew before how tiring it was to run around in the woods with your hands cuffed behind your back. They passed an old freezer, riddled with shotgun pellets. A sizzling noise came from it.

"What's that sound?" Ruza said.

"Snake's nest, probably," said Maria, and they all went way around the freezer and kept on going.

The last twenty yards of the path was down a steep incline of loose rocks and leaves. The old ladies leaped down, as it seemed to Magaracz, like a pair of ancient flying squirrels, lightly swinging between saplings. He came down in a sort of run to keep his legs under him, bouncing off trees to break his speed. At the bottom he sat down abruptly.

Gilmore Nash was stretched across the trail, snoring on a tarpaulin.

Just ahead was a house, Monica Nash's place, Magaracz realized. A track of scuffed earth showed where Gilmore Nash or something of similar size and weight had been dragged from the back door.

Monica sat on a stump nearby, sunning herself maybe, or just taking the morning air. A little pile of cigarette butts was by her feet.

"Hi," she said.

"Take cover," said Maria. "There are men with guns after us, and they've got the high ground."

"Guns?" said Monica.

"Can we use the phone?" said Magaracz.

"Oh, yes, come right inside. Sorry the place is such a mess."

Magaracz got lucky. In the basement workshop, hung up neatly, was a huge supply of tools, including a pair of cutters. While the old ladies called the cops and the FBI, Monica was able to use the cutters to part his handcuffs with a single stroke. Two Dobermans watched them from the corner.

"Gilmore's dogs," said Monica. "Scott and Henry will be happy to see them. Stay, boys." She led him upstairs to the phone and he called Ethel.

Ethel was very angry.

"I thought when you quit being a private detective that would be the end of this all-night stuff," she said.

"I'm sorry, honey."

"I didn't get a wink of sleep last night. Do you want to know what movies were on? Boring movies. I went off my diet."

"Did you eat the cheesecake?"

"I ate the cheesecake, Nick. Where are you?"

"I'm at Monica Nash's house," he said, regretting it instantly.

"What!"

"It's all right, I just got here. I've been locked up in a cellar with the Hedervary sisters. Listen, I'll make it up to you. Take the bus into town and meet me at Lorenzo's Steak House at noon. I'll buy you lunch." They said good-bye and hung up.

Then he had to dive for the floor, because someone was shooting through the windows, maybe fifteen or twenty rounds, pow-pow-pow.

The gunfire stopped. In the distance, but coming

closer, a siren wailed. Thumps and bangs sounded, and a car started up. Slowly the detective raised his head.

"You ladies all right?" he called.

All three voices answered yes. He got up and went into the kitchen.

Monica thought her house was a mess before, but it was nothing compared to this. Broken glass was everywhere, pieces of cups and plates covered the floor and counters. Stuff on the shelves had been shot. A stream of cornmeal poured from the side of a five-pound bag and slowly made a little yellow pile on the tile floor.

The ladies themselves were in a heap, with Monica on the bottom. "I got hit," said Maria as they untangled themselves. "Good thing I was wearing this vest. Ugh! I feel as though I'd been kicked by a horse."

"Will you be okay?" said Magaracz. She got to her feet stiffly.

"I think I'd better lie down for a while," she said, and staggered to the living room, glass and pottery crunching under her oxfords.

"They're gone, are they?" Ruza said. "I heard a car start." Monica got up and ran to the window.

"Oh, piss," she said. Tears welled in her eyes. "They took him."

In a cloud of flying dirt and gravel three police cars came screaming into the driveway and disgorged every law officer in Titusville. Special Agent Lucas himself drove up in a small black American car such as a self-effacing lawman or a midwestern Methodist minister might drive.

More and more Magaracz was overwhelmed by the feeling that this whole caper was the work of forces

120

from outside Trenton. It was a matter of style. Sure, Trenton had bad guys. They would rob you, or climb in your window and take your TV, or sell drugs to your kids, and if they wanted you dead they'd shoot you and leave your body in the trunk of a stolen car in the remote lot of Philadelphia airport. But they wouldn't dress up in fatigues and try to convert you to their way of life.

And Trenton had law officers. But they were normal people you'd want to drink a beer with, like his brother-in-law Fennuccio, not like this weirdo in the raincoat who came from Washington and had a stiff upper lip.

Clearly this was a case of Trentonians being corrupted by outside agitators.

"Magaracz," said Lucas, evidently in a rage. Magaracz wondered if he flared his nostrils like that on purpose or if it was involuntary. "Weren't you asked to leave this case alone?"

"The case wouldn't leave me alone," Magaracz said. "I was willing." The local cops were questioning the Hedervarys. Magaracz went into the kitchen.

Monica Nash was completely dejected. Before his eyes she seemed to have aged ten years. "I can't find the broom," she said.

"I saw it in the cellar," he said, patting her shoulder.

She brushed the debris off a kitchen chair, sat down, and put her head in her hands.

"I was so looking forward to being a real widow."

Oh? he thought. But he said, "You can always be a divorcée. A year and a half of separation is all you need in this state, that and a lawyer."

"That's right. I can talk to my boss, Mr. Lockman, about it. I won't even have to . . ." She stared into

121

space a long time without saying anything, then she looked at the detective.

"You have something else you want to tell me," he guessed.

"There's a hundred and forty-three pints of Drano in an old freezer up the hill in the woods," she said.

"Could be dangerous," he said. "What if the kids get into it?"

"That's what I was thinking. What do you think I should do?"

"Call the Department of Environmental Protection," he said. "They'll get somebody out here first thing tomorrow. Let me know if they give you any trouble. I know a guy over there. In the meantime keep the kids away from it."

"Thanks," she said with a dazzling smile. "I knew I could count on you for help." She went down to get the broom. What made her think she could count on him for help? Maybe if things had worked out differently she would have been coming to him with a sack of bones: "Here. I knew I could count on your help."

The cops came into the kitchen. "We're going over to the Bosnian Club now. If you want a ride to your car we'll take you."

He said, "Sure," and when Monica came back upstairs with her cleaning tools he told her good-bye and good luck. She stood in the doorway as they got in the police cars, holding the dustpan aloft and waving.

As they pulled out of her driveway there came through the windows a great rattling and tinkling, as Monica Nash began to clean up her house.

SIXTEEN

THERE WAS A new guard on the gate at the club, a uniformed policeman this time, and marked and unmarked law enforcement vehicles from every level of government were parked all over the yard. Magaracz noticed that the official Bosnian Club van was not among them. He was pretty sure it had been there when he and the Hedervarys were escaping. He mentioned it to Special Agent Lucas.

Lucas beckoned to a guy who proved to be a State Police lieutenant. "Describe the van to him," he said to Magaracz. "You'll want to put out a bulletin on this, Feeny. Bosnian Club van."

Outside the gates, a pearl-gray stretch limousine rolled to a stop and four sleek men in suits and ties got out.

"Jesus, now what," muttered the lieutenant.

It was two men from the New Zinderneuf Trap Rock Company and their lawyers.

"Seems to be something going on here," said one of them. "Is Dr. Herman Eckes around? We have an appointment to meet with him and sign some papers."

Maria Hedervary came striding up. She had taken

off the vest, and seemed completely recovered from the shock of being hit by a bullet, except for an almost imperceptible reluctance to use her left arm. She stepped outside the gate, put out her right hand, and said, "How do you do, I'm Maria Hedervary. Perhaps I can help you. Dr. Eckes has passed away; my sister and I are the owners now." The man who had spoken shook hands with her, and gave her an oily smile. Ruza came out, and they all disappeared with a flutter into the limousine.

Magaracz described the van to the lieutenant. "I'll get on the radio with this," he said. He got into his car and began to broadcast the description.

There was an explosion in the woods. A rabbit came tearing out of there and went across the parking yard like a seventy-five-millimeter shell.

A cloud of gray smoke drifted out of the woods toward them, its smell sharp and familiar, reminding Magaracz of his days in the service. "Mines, maybe," he said.

"And get them to send the bomb squad out," the lieutenant added to the dispatcher.

The Hedervarys emerged from the limousine, having struck a satisfactory bargain. "Mr. Magaracz," Maria said, "they offered us enough for this place to keep us in comfort in Sun City, Arizona, for as long as we live." There was rye whiskey on her breath.

"Did they ply you ladies with alcohol?" asked Magaracz.

"Oh, yes. There's a bar in there."

"Make sure you talk it all over with your lawyer before you sign anything," Magaracz advised.

"Excuse me, miss, we'd like to ask you a few questions," the lieutenant said. He took them to the door of the basement. "Is this cellar where you ladies were held prisoner?"

"Why, yes, it is, but . . ."

"But what?"

"I wonder what could have happened," she said, "to all those crates of dynamite that were down here?"

Parked down the old back road in Monica's car, Dwayne, the Ace, and young Robert Stout were trying to wake Gilmore up while three other young men in fatigues and short haircuts stood around the car nervously.

"What's wrong with him? You think he's dying?"

"Look at that lump on his head."

"His breath smells, my friend," said the Ace. "Personally I'd say he was drugged, perhaps struck on the head afterwards. Get me some water from the brook."

They brought water in a paper cup and bathed his face with a sweatsock. He moaned and stirred.

"Wake up, Gil."

"It's us! Your friends!"

"What happened?" he said.

"Evidently your wife assaulted you," said the Ace.

"Assaulted — ?"

"The doctor is dead, Gil, and so is Kenny. Joe Batt was shot. We don't think he made it."

"I'll ask you again," said Nash, sitting up and glaring at them. "What happened?"

"There was some trouble," Dwayne said.

They all began to talk at him.

"We need you."

"For one last attack on the State."

"All the dynamite is in the car."

"We're going to smash Trenton."

Gilmore Nash looked around at their eager young faces and realized that they expected him to lead them now. He sighed. "All right," he said. "What you need is a plan."

"Yes," they agreed.

"Well, what are our resources?"

Ace Jeder said, "We have two Smith and Wessons, a handful of ammo, eight MAC Tens that don't work, two vehicles, a crate and a half of dynamite, and there are seven of us left."

"Did you get the radio-control device?" Nash said.

"Where was it?" said Dwayne.

"I was carrying it, the last I remember," said Nash.

"It looked like a little boombox, right?" said the Ace. "We got it. It's in the car."

"Good. Now, what are our objectives?"

"Smash the State!" said Dwayne.

"Oh, come on," Gilmore Nash said.

"Surely it will be enough," said the Ace, "just to get the State off our backs. Some government is necessary for an orderly society."

"I want to kill the Governor," said Dwayne. "Do you know they were going to revoke my driver's license? A free man ought to be able to drive."

"But that was before, Dwayne," said Nash. "They can't touch you now. As far as the Governor knows, you don't exist."

"I want him to know I exist," said Dwayne. "I want it to be the last thing he knows, too."

126

"Well, okay," said Nash. "Dwayne wants the Governor. I want the Tax building. Any other goals?"

"I'd kind of like to get out of this alive," said Bob Stout.

"Pussy," muttered Dwayne.

"Don't forget this," Ace Jeder said, pulling a cassette tape out of his pocket. "It's the doc's tape. A powerful propaganda weapon."

They all looked at the tape.

"What did he say on it?" Dwayne asked.

"He explained everything," the Ace said. "It's enormously persuasive. No one can listen to it without feeling drawn to our cause."

"Well, then," said Nash, "by all means let's be sure the whole world hears it."

Superior Court Judge Abraham Burney (retired) went out to look in his mailbox once again. If his pension check wasn't there today it would be time to make some phone calls. He was almost beside the road when he heard low, earnest voices coming from the field next to his property. Judge Burney peered cautiously over the top of his unkempt privet hedge.

There in a circle sat a small force of paramilitary personnel, waving their weapons in the air and drawing lines in the dirt.

The judge took a good long look at them. The uniforms, first of all, didn't look quite like anything legitimate that he knew of. There was something bogus about their demeanor, too, as if they had learned it on TV. Then there was the man who appeared to be their leader. He looked like a convict as much as anything else.

"One o'clock," the leader said. "It's now eleven thirty-two." They all fiddled with their watches. *Robbers*, thought the judge. Probably planning an assault on the neighborhood.

Judge Burney faded quietly back into his garden, leaving the mail, if any, in the box, and went indoors and called the police.

But before the police could get there the LFD had boarded their vehicles and embarked for glory.

SEVENTEEN

THE MAN THAT Maria Hedervary shot in the woods was still alive when they found him. They took him to Mercer Medical Center for emergency surgery. Lieutenant Frank Fennuccio told his brother-in-law about it, and offered to meet him there.

"He should be coming out of the recovery room any minute now, Nick. Let's go see if we can question him." They went in the emergency entrance and up the back elevator. The nurse in Intensive Care asked for their passes to see the patient.

"I'm a police officer," Fennuccio said sternly. "We're here about a very important murder case." She stared at them, wide-eyed, and told them not to take long or get the patient overexcited. Life and death were ordinary matters here, but murder was still unusual.

The patient was propped up in bed, stuck full of tubes and all bandaged. His color was ghastly. Nevertheless Magaracz recognized his old schoolfellow Joe Batt.

"Joey," said Magaracz, "how do you feel?" It was a dumb question.

"Bad," the funeral director replied. His voice sounded strange because of the oxygen tube in his nose, but it

129

was clear enough for them to understand what he was saying.

"This is my brother-in-law, Frank Fennuccio," said Magaracz. "He's with the Trenton Police Department, and he wants to ask you some questions."

"It was all Herman Eckes's work," said Batt, gesturing feebly with his free hand. Dark blood dripped slowly into a plastic tube that snaked under some bandages into his arm. "We went along with what he said. He seemed to know what he was doing." A readout on the wall above Batt's head showed numbers constantly changing up and down, his heart rate, or his pulse, something. *You could use it for a lie detector,* Magaracz thought. *If you knew how to detect lies.* But they would need some sort of sweat sensor with it. Batt was in fact sweating profusely. He was in a lot of pain, probably. A bag of pee with a tube leading out from under the covers hung by the bedside. Maybe they could measure that. If they asked him a question and he filled up the bag some more, they would know they were onto something.

But Batt was not withholding or covering up anything now. He was singing like a birdie.

"He got all these guys from ads in magazines, and then if he thought they were all right he would sign their death certificates for an additional fee and I would take care of the rest of it. Most times he just kept their five dollars."

"Fake cremations," said Magaracz.

"Why not? What business is it of the government whether a man is alive or dead?" The flickering pulse rate went up and up. Batt began to cough. It hurt him.

130

"Take it easy," said Fennuccio. "Take it easy. It's okay."

Batt became more calm, and asked for a cloth to mop his brow. It was brought to him. "Eckes is dead now," he said. "They blew him up. That little fartsack Dwayne had the nerve to give me a cyanide capsule after I was wounded. I didn't take it, or else I'd be dead too."

Fennuccio said, "Take it easy."

"Dwayne was one of the ones that Herman kept."

"Kept?"

"Some of them he'd sign their death certificates and they'd go away and live some other life in a different place. It was wonderful for them." He closed his eyes, and after a while they thought he'd fallen asleep or passed out.

Then he said in a faraway voice, "But some he would keep, to carry on the work of the LFD."

"The LFD?" they repeated.

"The League of the Free Dead, they called themselves."

"Murchison, Ritter, Harkness, and Stout," said Magaracz.

"Murchison and Stout, anyway," Batt replied. "Ritter and Harkness went away, we never knew where. And of course Gil Nash and that kid who calls himself Ace Jeder, and a few others."

"What does this group have to do with the Posse Comitatus?" asked Fennuccio.

"Sort of a splinter group," said Batt. "The Posse was beginning to get awfully . . . liberal. . . ." He drifted away again.

Fennuccio said, "See if you can wake him up long

131

enough to get the names and descriptions of the LFD guys."

Magaracz said, "Wait a minute. I'm trying to think. Cyanide capsules."

"Yeah, how about that. Is that crazy, or what? You know, as it is he might not make it. Then to go and give him —"

"No, Fennuch, listen. I was thinking about the so-called heart attack of Oswald Badger."

"You mean —"

"I remember Dr. Eckes bending over him, loosening his tongue. But what if he wasn't doing that at all. What if he was removing a capsule —"

"Which Badger had already bitten on," Fennuccio said.

"Because they told him it was some drug," Magaracz continued, "that would give him heart attack symptoms so he could pretend to die."

"That's a weird idea, Nick," Fennuccio said.

"No," said Magaracz. "He was all packed. I found his bag under the back steps of the clubhouse just before they got me. I bet it's still there. He was all ready to join the gang with his tiny little combat boots and everything. That's why he threw away his pants."

The nurse came and told them to get out. They were making noise and the patients were trying to rest.

In the hall they met old Mrs. Batt. She glared at Magaracz.

"So you're a policeman," she said to him. "You know, you could have told me my son was in trouble. We might have avoided all this." She gestured toward the door to the Intensive Care Unit.

"I'm sorry," Magaracz said miserably. "But it's not like he was a little kid." Batt was fifty, kind of old to be straightened out by his mother, but probably she was right, he should have told her. The old lady was crying. Weeping women.

"And you can tell your friend Miss Hedervary that we intend to prosecute to the fullest extent of the law. If those women had ever had any children of their own they would have more feeling than to be attacking other people's."

Fennuccio cleared his throat. "Mrs. Batt, I need to ask you something," he said. "Is Oswald Badger still in your cooler?"

"Yes, he is."

"We're going to have to do an autopsy on him. I hope it doesn't inconvenience you too much," he said.

"Not at all. Go right ahead. Excuse me." She went through the doors to Intensive Care to sit with her son.

Fennuccio and Magaracz continued their conversation about the death of Badger, keeping their voices down.

"They knew he was a tax man," Magaracz speculated, "from reading Monica Nash's mail. She says she never got that letter from him. Then when he turned up as a candidate for the LFD they figured him for a government plant."

"Do you think he was?" said Fennuccio. "I mean, do you think maybe on his own, he . . ."

"No way of knowing," said Magaracz. "We could always search his house. Maybe he left a note or something." But probably not.

"Doesn't really matter," Fennuccio said. "What's important is who are the other guys, and what are they going to try next."

A mental picture flashed into Magaracz's mind of

133

the kid in the Bergenfield High sweatshirt who had followed him. "Bergenfield," he said. "Right." The family waiting room had a phone in it; as soon as somebody's anxious relative stopped using it he put in all his change and made a call to Myra Toddhunter.

"You again," she said.

"Sorry to disturb you, Mrs. Toddhunter, but I have to ask you one thing. Could you give me a physical description of your son?"

"A physical description?"

"Yeah. Was he tall, short, dark, fair . . . did he have, like, a big nose, for instance. . . ."

Myra Toddhunter groaned. *So, okay*, Magaracz thought, *maybe I wasn't very tactful*. She said, "He wanted to have it altered when he was fifteen. We thought it irrational at the time. Now that I remember, that was when he started seeing the psychiatrist. I've often thought that if only . . ."

"Dark hair? Tall?"

"Why, yes."

"Stoop-shouldered?"

"You could say so, but . . . Mr. Magaracz, what are you driving at?"

Then Magaracz had to tell her that the kid was alive, and she cried at him again and hung up.

Old Mrs. Batt put her head out of the door to Intensive Care. "Mister policeman," she said.

"Yeah," said both men in unison.

"My son has something he wants to tell you." They rushed in. Another deathbed confession?

Pale, trembling, Batt sat up a little. His pulse rate was flashing and clicking.

"They're going to blow up Taxation today," said Joseph Batt.

EIGHTEEN

"LET'S STOP AND get a hoagie at Frankie J's, Nick. I can't fight crime on an empty stomach." Magaracz figured it was okay. Fennuch had called the other cops from the hospital. Whatever was going on downtown, they could handle it. For Fennuch and Nick it was time to eat.

They had to park on Rutgers Place, a short cul-de-sac that went down a little hill to the Carteret Arms Apartments. Tenants of the Carteret Arms included a radio station, a restaurant, a convenience store, a beauty parlor, several doctors' offices, and a large number of well-off senior citizens. All had their own parking places in the barbed-wire-enclosed lot, which left the street free for the public. There was a large, posh lobby, and a full-time doorman. The parking places in front of the door were best. The possibility of being seen by the doorman was a deterrent to thieves and vandals.

But the choice parking places were taken, so Magaracz had to drive down and loop around. By good luck someone was pulling out as he came back up Rutgers Place. He pulled in and parked. Then he and Fennuccio dodged the noontime traffic on State Street to go get their hoagies.

135

They had to squeeze between a run-down car and a van with a broken side window, illegally parked, to reach Frankie J's. The smell of onions and oregano inside was pungent. "Geez, I'm hungry," said Magaracz. He had missed his breakfast. Fennuccio ordered two hoagies with everything on them.

"Make those to go," said Magaracz.

"What to go," said Fennuccio. "I want to sit down and eat my sandwich."

But Magaracz had suddenly realized that the van outside was the Bosnians'. "To go," he said. "It seems the four winds have blown into town."

"What?" said his brother-in-law.

"We'll come back for the sandwiches," Magaracz said. "Come on, that van out there with the broken window belongs to the Bosnian Club. I know that bumper sticker with the gun on it."

"We'll stake it out," said Fennuccio. "Be reasonable. All I had this morning was toast and coffee." But then he saw the men from the club creeping down Rutgers Place, toting weapons, and he knew that something had to be done about them right away.

The doorman of the Carteret Arms looked up from his morning paper to see a party of armed commandos raiding his lobby. Tramping in step, the LFD swooped in the door and demanded to know where the radio station was.

"Nine," the doorman said, gaping at them. As gray-haired ladies lounging in the lobby stared at them in horror, the men crammed themselves into the first elevator that stopped for them. The door slid shut.

Magaracz and Fennuccio came running in.

"Hey, did a bunch of guys with Uzis come in here just now?"

"Yeah, man. They took the elevator. They're going up to the radio station on the ninth floor."

"Can you stop it between floors?" said Magaracz.

"What for?"

"Just do it," said Fennuccio, showing his police badge.

In his wife's car a few blocks away, Gilmore Nash was running through the plan one more time for Dwayne. "It's very simple. You run the car up onto the State House steps. With all the dynamite in the trunk probably it'll take out the Governor and half the legislators. I'll be down the street setting off the radio-controlled charges in the Tax building with this thing." He brandished the radio-control device.

Dwayne narrowed his eyes. "But wait a minute. That looks like I'd get killed for sure."

"No. No. What you do is go down State Street, swerve toward the steps, and then jump out and roll behind some shelter just at the last minute."

"What shelter?"

"There's a concrete curb across the street big enough to get behind. I've got this all reconnoitered." It was a lie, but so what. With Sergeant Rock, here, out of the way Gilmore would be free to go west or do whatever he wanted to.

"You're sure?"

"Would I lie to you?"

"Well . . . okay," said Dwayne.

Since the Carteret Arms was on the outskirts of the usual lunchtime clog of traffic, massive numbers of policemen of all kinds had no trouble getting there right away and relieving Fennuccio and Magaracz of their vigil by the elevator. The LFD guys were stuck between floors, all right, and since it was not known what they meant to do, or whether they had any explosives with them, the authorities evacuated the building and surrounded the elevator, waiting.

Magaracz and Fennuccio picked up their hoagies and headed uptown, munching and dribbling oil as they went. No point in taking the car, Magaracz remarked.

"We can walk it faster than we can find a place to park," agreed Fennuccio. Indeed they were walking very fast.

"Oh, hell," said Magaracz. "Ethel."

"What about her?"

"I promised to meet her at Lorenzo's at noon."

"Too late now," Fennuccio said. "It's twenty minutes of one."

There was a big noontime demonstration going on in front of the State House. About a hundred demonstrators were shuffling around in a circle carrying mysterious and ambiguous hand-lettered placards. A muscular young fellow stood on the steps of the State House pumping his arm and leading them in an unintelligible chant.

LEADER: What do we WANT?
PEOPLE: HUFFLE!
LEADER: When do we WANT it?
PEOPLE: WAH!

This was a familiar sight on State Street, although not as frequent as it used to be before most of the citizens had either achieved huffle or succumbed to despair.

138

The chief effect of demonstrations was to tie up traffic and make it hard for state workers to get to lunch. Depending on how rowdy the demonstrators were expected to be, one or more city cops might be on duty to bolster the forces of the Capitol Police. This was a class A demonstration, Magaracz observed; six of the women were carrying a coffin swathed in black crepe paper, always a sign of serious purpose in a demonstration, and the city had sent two police officers.

Fennuccio spoke to the city cops.

The city cops spoke to the Capitol Police.

The Capitol Police went up to the leader, and in low voices they spoke to him.

His frown of noble class resentment became a scowl of outrage. Magaracz could hear him saying, "No, man. Where do you get off? We have a permit."

They spoke to him some more, still in low voices, and gestured toward the Taxation building and then at the other side of State Street.

The demonstrators stopped walking and watched the group on the State House steps. Some muttered angrily.

The leader looked startled, and glanced toward the Taxation building with apprehension.

"Hey, man! What's going on?" someone in the crowd demanded.

The matrons put the coffin down and stood belligerently with hands on hips.

A newspaper photographer began to dance around the outskirts of the demonstration, trying for art shots.

"People!" the leader boomed. "These gentlemen have asked us to move across the street!"

"Hell, no! We won't go!" someone said, and the crowd took up the chant.

"No, listen, seriously," the leader called, but it was in vain. Nobody listened.

It was fourteen minutes to one.

There were more Capitol Police manning and womaning the barricades at the corner of West State and Willow streets. Black and white striped sawhorses that said "POLICE" closed off West State Street to keep the lunchtime crowds from running over the demonstrators.

It presented a problem for Dwayne. Sure, he could have crashed the barricade, but somehow he felt that such an act would draw undue attention to him before he could complete his work.

"Look at this crowd, Gil. How am I gonna get near the State House steps? I think we should try this again tomorrow."

"Listen, you cretin," said Nash. "This operation is supposed to be a coordinated effort. They didn't teach you guys much at that camp, did they? We're synchronizing this attack with the assault on the radio station, remember? Right this very minute the others are getting ready to deliver Dr. Eckes's dying message to the world. You can be a part of that, Dwayne, if you'll only get your ass in gear."

"How?"

Gilmore Nash sighed. "Go up around by Capitol Alley," he said.

"Where's that?"

"It goes behind the houses across the street from the State House. Go across State Street, make the first

140

left, go up the alley, left again, and you'll come right out by the State House Annex. From there you turn left on State Street and it's a straight shot to the State House steps."

"How long will it take to get around that way?" asked Dwayne.

"Shouldn't take more than a couple of minutes. Why?"

"I want to be sure and get there exactly at one."

"Something wrong with your watch?"

"Yeah. It stopped. I think the battery's dead."

Nash looked at his own watch. "Stay here for two minutes," he said. "Then go."

"Two minutes?"

"Yeah. Count to a hundred and twenty, one thousand one, one thousand two. I'll see you." *In hell*, he thought, as he left the car and slipped away into the crowd.

It was just about then that the bomb threat finally found its way through channels to the Taxation building.

The receptionist in the downstairs lobby got the call. After a hasty conference with the Capitol Police officer on duty there she pulled the fire alarm. Everyone thought it was a drill.

The computer room was still embroiled in the task of hand-cataloguing all the tapes. Tape reels were spread over every flat surface, while the operators read their labels one after the other, visually first and then electronically, trying to find out what system each belonged to before it could be accidentally scratched. When the alarm went off they got up and

141

made for the door with relief and delight. But Howard Ucksby snarled, "Did I say you guys could go? You stay here."

"The fire alarm is going off," said Rob Fenkis.

"I don't care if the whole place burns down," said Ucksby. "Nobody leaves here until these tapes are straightened out."

Everywhere else in the building the state employees went out into the halls and lined up in orderly fashion (Arthur Pacewick, Nick's boss, was among them), waiting for the office fire marshals to show up and tell them what to do next. Almost everyone was out to lunch, the fire marshals too.

The more independent state workers went down the stairs and out the front door, defying standing instructions. There was an enormous crowd out there. Traffic was backed up for blocks because of the demonstration. Even pedestrians could scarcely move around. In the distance, sirens screamed and horns blared as fire trucks tried to get through.

Magaracz had to struggle against a surging tide of bodies to approach his office building. "Lemmings swimming upstream," said a woman beside him. But he was not daunted. He had left his dad's gold watch in his desk drawer.

NINETEEN

THE HESSIAN BARRACKS looked to Gilmore Nash as though it could easily withstand any number of hits on the neighboring buildings. A class of second-graders from Englewood Cliffs was filing out to board their chartered bus. Nash threaded his way among them into the building.

The children gave him strange looks as he passed. Some stared, some glanced at him and looked away politely. It was true that he was not dressed or groomed for town, true that his encounter with Monica, which he could neither remember nor imagine, seemed to have left lumps of mud in his hair and beard. But bathing could wait; after he had done what he came for, then a bath, maybe. He had to do this now, had to, the way you have to scratch an itch.

He stepped into the cool building. A woman looked up from a desk at him, her face a polite mask. "I'd like to see the barracks, if I may," he said. "What's the admission?" He was in a large, airy space with a balcony over it and many windows. What he really needed was some well-protected hole.

She told him the price and he paid it, peeling money off a roll he kept in his back pocket. No doubt the basement of this place would make an excellent bunker.

"If you'll wait until one o'clock" — the lady smiled at him — "we'll be starting another guided tour."

He could not wait until one o'clock. "No thanks," he said. "I'll guide myself, if it's all the same to you."

"I'll have to ask you to keep your tape player turned off," she said, gesturing toward the radio-control apparatus under his arm.

"I promise you won't hear a sound from it," he said.

Outside, his engine idling in front of the Taxation building, Dwayne was counting: "One thousand ninety-nine, one thousand a hundred, one thousand a hundred one . . ."

Magaracz came wading through the crowd toward the Taxation building. When he reached the curbstone in front, he found Ruth Ann Walker and another one of the local crazies sitting there, old friends of his since the time he went under cover as a derelict.

"Hello, sweetie," said Ruth Ann, gazing at him mournfully over the tops of her two pairs of glasses.

"Hiya, Ruth Ann!" said Magaracz. "Nice day! How's it going, Burt?" He sat down with them on the curb. "You out for good now?"

"Day pass," said Burt.

"Lots of people here today," Ruth Ann said.

"It's kind of nice," said Burt. "All those faces. Say, do you think Trenton is going to turn around?"

Somebody was always asking Magaracz if Trenton was going to turn around. He always said, "Sure," and he said it now.

"Have you got a cigarette, honey?" said Ruth Ann. "And one for my boyfriend here."

He gave her a cigarette, and looked up, and there was Ethel. She was waiting for him outside the Tax

144

building just so she could give him that look of reproach in person.

"I sat there for twenty minutes, Nick, and then I thought, well, as often as I ever get out, I might as well enjoy this, so I had some calamari and scungilli, and then I ordered their best steak."

"Was it good?"

"Very good. I saved you some."

"Um — I hope you had enough money on you — I know they don't take cards."

"It's okay. I was able to handle it."

"I'll make it up to you."

"I know," she said, in a voice that filled him with foreboding. Then he saw the car.

It was none other than a light gray fifty-seven Studebaker with a big dent in the right rear fender and a failed inspection sticker, idling at the curbside. The guy at the wheel, one of the ones who had chased Magaracz and the Hedervarys through the woods, was mumbling to himself.

"Hey, Ethel. You got a potato on you?" Magaracz said.

"You know perfectly well that all I have on me is this piece of steak."

"Let me have it."

"What for?" she said.

"The fate of the entire city could depend on it."

"But that's for our supper tonight."

"Gimme it."

"Nick!"

He seized the doggie bag over Ethel's protests and thrust the gobbet of juicy steak into the exhaust pipe of the Studebaker before the hungry eyes of Ruth Ann and Burt.

"Nick!!"

"Hey, is that steak?" said Burt. "I ain't seen steak like that in ten years."

"Don't say anything," Magaracz whispered. "We're saving the city of Trenton."

Dwayne counted to one thousand a hundred and twenty, put the car in gear, and gunned the engine. It died. He tried to restart it. No go. He looked up; the Taxation building towered over his head, precariously as it seemed to him, with four minutes left to go before Gilmore Nash would set off his explosive devices. He looked around. Blue uniforms seemed to be converging on his car. He scrambled out and began to run.

The cops jumped on him and got him down before he reached the corner. He could see a little lump of putty in the wall of the Tax building almost by his head. That would be covering one of Gilmore Nash's bombs. "Let me go! Not here! Not here!" he screamed. "A guy is gonna blow up this building at one o'clock!"

They handcuffed him and threw him in the back of the police van, and then they rushed inside to clear the people out.

"One o'clock. Geez. What time have you got, Ethel?"

"Five of," she said. "It might not be right."

"Somebody has to find Gilmore Nash. Where would you go if you were going to blow up a building?"

"Someplace where it wouldn't fall on me," she said.

They looked up; they looked down; they looked all around. The Taxation building towered over them. "Not here," he said.

"The building next door?"

"They tore that down last week, Ethel."

146

"Across the street, then," she said. "Some public place where they would let him in."

"The Hessian Barracks," said Magaracz.

They ran across the street to the Hessian Barracks. Ruth Ann Walker came trailing after them, the soles of her shoes flapping. "About that steak," she called. "You wouldn't happen to have . . ."

Magaracz asked the lady at the desk inside, "Have you seen a grubby-looking guy with a beard? About thirty-five? Carrying something, a piece of equipment?"

"Yes," she said; "he went that way." She pointed to the cellar stairs.

"I gotta go down there and get him," Magaracz said. "Damn it, Ethel, my father's gold watch is in the Tax building."

"But, Nick, the cops will be here in two minutes."

"We don't have two minutes. I've got to go down there myself and get that son of a bitch."

"Nick, can you take him? I mean, no offense, but he's a killer."

"I dunno, Ethel," said Nick. "Probably not if he knows I'm coming. Maybe I could if there was a distraction of some kind."

"Oh, that's easy," said Ethel. "Come on, Ruth Ann," and she took her by the hand and ran out.

From outside the computer room came the sound of sirens howling and feet moving as if in panic. Somebody thumped on the door and hollered. The door was too thick to make out what they said. The computer operators were beginning to suspect that there was some sort of real emergency, perhaps involving danger to themselves. They were getting edgy. Without

147

consciously reaching for it, Russ Woodshard found a cigarette in his hands. Ucksby was on his case before he could put it away.

"Hey, listen, pea-brain," began the supervisor's standard cigarette lecture. They had all heard it a hundred times. It ended with him telling them how many years of their pay it would cost to recharge the Halon system.

This time, though, Ucksby didn't finish the talk. Before he was halfway through there was a loud bang, and a piece of the wall flew out, striking him on the head. He fell to the floor, unconscious.

"How about that!" Rob Fenkis said.

"Hey, what did you do to him?" asked another operator.

"Nothin'," Woodshard said. "The wall did it."

The Halon alarm went off, a hideous clanging. There was a hissing sound as the gas was released into the computer room. They could feel it puddling on the floor, a coldness rising past their ankles.

"Let's get the hell out of here."

"Wait," said Woodshard. "Help me carry Ucksby."

"Leave him," Fenkis advised.

"No, I can't leave him. Get his feet."

"Shit," said Fenkis. But he got his feet, and they struggled out in time to keep from being smothered.

Nash tried to remember the sequence of signals that would bring the Taxation building down. The cellar was just what he'd hoped for, a low-ceilinged hole with stout stone walls and a window that let in just enough light for him to see what he was doing with the radio control. Used for storage, the cellar was full of boxes of artifacts.

The window faced away from the Tax building and toward the State House lawn, lessening the chance of flying glass even from Dwayne's efforts, since the steps of the State House were on the other side of that building. Excellent place. Too low to stand up in, so he crouched down on his hunkers, facing the stairs with the Smith and Wesson across his knees in case of unwelcome company.

A muffled BOOM! told him that he was beginning to get the right frequencies at last. Then the rattle of stones on the cellar window suggested he had really shaken something loose.

He looked around to see what sort of pebbles they might be, but it was fingernails rattling.

Two madwomen were scratching on the cellar window of the Hessian Barracks.

Down on their elbows and knees in the dirt, they seemed to be having some sort of contest as to which of them could present the most grotesque appearance. They crossed their eyes, they pulled on the flesh of their faces, they smeared their noses back and forth on the glass. The one in the black wig took it and skewed it forward over her face, then tucked her hands in her armpits and howled like a dog. The other one pushed up her nose, pulled down her lower eyelids till you could see the red, rolled her tongue around and yodeled "Walalala!" in a loud voice.

Then the first one mashed her face against the glass and tried to talk through it, producing a bizarre vibration, and the second one started to take off her —

But that was all he knew.

Guys like Gilmore Nash, Magaracz reflected, *you get 'em from behind whenever you can.* He put down the

149

colonial musket, which had served the cause of true freedom once again, this time as a cudgel. There was an on-off switch on the radio-control box. Magaracz turned it off.

He waved and beckoned to the women. Ethel stopped making faces and looked relieved, but Ruth Ann was just beginning to get into it. Ethel had to pull her away by the arm.

They went around and came inside about the same time that the cops arrived, Ethel's brother Fennuch and a couple of strangers in SWAT suits. Magaracz heard them talking to the woman at the door, who sounded upset. Then they all came down the cellar steps.

"That's him, is it?" said one of the SWAT guys. "He don't look so dangerous."

"Take it from me," said Magaracz. "He's dangerous."

There was more noise upstairs, and a couple of volunteers from the Liberty Rescue Squad came down with a stretcher.

"Better tie him to it real tight," said the SWAT guy. "And watch him. Don't forget that other one who hijacked the ambulance last year."

The fellow from the rescue squad looked nervous and said he'd be careful. They lashed him down well. A rattlesnake with the strength of ten men could not have wiggled out.

"Nice work," said Magaracz to the women.

"I told your wife we ought to drop trou," Ruth Ann boomed.

"Nah, they wanted to take him alive," Magaracz said, as they carried Gilmore Nash up the stairs. The

SWAT guys went along. Probably he would get off on grounds of insanity; that seemed to be how these things went. Still, with any luck they would put him away for a good long stretch in the Forensic wing of Trenton Psychiatric.

And if he got out, so what? He hadn't seen who hit him.

"Ruth Ann," said Ethel, "let us buy you lunch."

"My boyfriend too?" Ruth Ann said.

"Him, too," said Ethel, "and a pack of cigarettes for each of you. I think you just saved Nick's life."

"Can we go to McDonald's and sit in the window?"

"We certainly can. Come on, Nick."

"I'll meet you there," he said. The women left. Fennuccio started upstairs too, with the radio-control apparatus in his hand, and Nick Magaracz told him for Christ's sake not to turn it on.

"Don't worry," Fennuccio said. "We're not even using radios or walkie-talkies till they get the explosives cleaned out of the Taxation building. The State Police Bomb Squad warned us about that."

"Did they get those other guys out of the elevator yet?" Magaracz asked Fennuccio.

"They're waiting for Myra Toddhunter."

Magaracz said, "No kidding."

The lady by the door gave them a nervous smile when they came upstairs, and told them to have a nice day; as soon as they were out the door, she followed after them and locked it behind her. All up and down the street, buildings were being evacuated. Magaracz thought, *It's okay, it's all safe now,* but maybe it wasn't, he didn't know.

"Yeah, Myra Toddhunter. She called the Governor

151

and told him you said her son was running with a paramilitary organization. He figured it must be the ones in the elevator, so he sent his private helicopter for her. He figures she can talk them out. Toddhunter was the leader, the doorman said."

"Some people will follow anybody," Magaracz said. "How about it? You want a Big Mac?"

EPILOGUE

THE LFD DECIDED not to have a final shootout in the elevator. No one had prepared them for it. Their sergeant in right-wing camp had spoken of subway fighting, and they had done some drilling in a big sewer pipe, but this situation was too vertical.

Besides, they were virtually unarmed. Gilmore Nash had taken one of the Smith and Wessons with him, and the other one only had three bullets in it. The Ace had failed to fix the MAC Tens after Maria Hedervary's sabotage. The troops were carrying them only for effect.

When at last the Ace got the trapdoor open and poked his head up through the top of the elevator, he found himself staring into two powerful spotlights and the shadowy faces of a phalanx of FBI men, bristling with weaponry. The tearstained face of his own mother was among them. At the sight of her he was unmanned completely, and gave himself up.

The customer who bought the real detonator from Fatman for a cable tuner was unable to make it work. In spite of Fatman's protestations that no guarantees were implied or intended, the customer felt that he

153

was entitled to redress, and stabbed Fatman in the shoulder.

Fatman was in the hospital for three weeks. The customer pulled five to ten in Trenton State Prison. Junkie Tyrone is still at large, so watch out where you park your car after dark.

A disk jockey at the radio station in the Carteret Arms obtained the doctor's tape, and played some of it over the air, with hoots of derision. Several other wing-nut organizations of the right and left demanded equal time.

Nick Magaracz continued to toil in the bowels of the faceless bureaucracy, but kept alive his dreams of going to work for private industry as an expert in industrial espionage. Computers, he felt, were the wave of the future. He took a course at Mercer County Community College and learned a lot of buzzwords. Sometimes he practiced them on Ethel.